ENGLISH IS NOT A MAGIC LANGUAGE

JACQUES POULIN

English is not a Magic Language

A NOVEL

TRANSLATED FROM THE FRENCH
BY SHEILA FISCHMAN

ESPLANADE
Books

THE FICTION SERIES AT VÉHICULE PRESS

Published with the generous assistance of the Canada Council for the Arts, the Canada Book Fund of the Department of Canadian Heritage, and the Société de développement des entreprises culturelles du Québec (SODEC).
We acknowledge the financial support of the Government of Canada through the National Translation Program for Book Publishing, an initiative of the *Roadmap for Canada's Official Languages 2013-2018: Education, Immigration, Communities*, for our translation activities.

Funded by the Government of Canada
Financé par le gouvernement du Canada

Esplanade Books editor: Dimitri Nasrallah
Cover design: David Drummond
Typeset in Minion by Simon Garamond
Printed by Marquis Printing Inc.

LIBRARY AND ARCHIVES CANADA CATALOGUING IN PUBLICATION

Poulin, Jacques, 1937-
[L'anglais n'est pas une langue magique. English]
English is not a magic language / Jacques Poulin ; translator, Sheila Fischman.

Translation of: L'anglais n'est pas une langue magique.
ISBN 978-1-55065-423-3 (paperback)

I. Fischman, Sheila, translator II. Title.
III. Title: L'anglais n'est pas une langue magique. English.

PS8531.O82A7213 2015   C843'.54   C2015-902721-7

Published by Véhicule Press, Montréal, Québec, Canada
vehiculepress.com
Distributed by LitDistCo in Canada | www.litdistco.ca
Distributed by IPG in the U.S. | www.ipgbook.com
Printed in Canada on FSC® certified paper.

MIX
Paper from
responsible sources
FSC® C103567

This story has been reviewed by some people
with infinite patience. – J.P.

Pierre Filion provided inestimable help at a critical time in the preparation of this translation and I thank him from the bottom of my heart. – S.F.

CONTENTS

Reading, almost as much as breathing,
is our essential function.

—ALBERTO MANGUEL
A History of Reading

1

Misunderstanding

TAKE ME, FOR INSTANCE. You don't know a thing about me. I am walking down rue Saint-Jean, you're sitting on the terrace of the Hobbit, and you don't even see me. I'm Jack's kid brother. Even though I didn't study literature as he did, I get by in life very well. I am a reader on demand, that's my profession. And I have all kinds of adventures.

Only yesterday, the phone rang. It was eight p.m.

"Hello?"

"Are you the reader?" asked a woman's voice.

"Yes, I am."

"May I have an appointment?"

"Certainly."

Her voice was soft and lilting when she said the word appointment, so I paid close attention to what she was saying:

"Will you come to my house?"

"Sure," I said. "What day would you like?"

There was a moment's silence.

"Could you come tomorrow night?"

"Certainly. Say eight o'clock?"

She gave me an address and a door code.

The house was on the edge of the Plains of Abraham, on rue de Bernières. I jotted her instructions in my datebook, then I waited. Sometimes clients mention what they would like to listen to, or the name of the author. If they say nothing I don't make suggestions: it's a sign that they enjoy surprises.

The woman remained silent. Under normal circumstances, after the usual goodbyes I would have hung up. This time though I wanted to hear that little music of hers again.

"Is there anything in particular you'd like?"

"What we talk about when we talk about love."

I was speechless. It took me a few seconds to pull myself together and figure out how to end the conversation. Later, I realized my mistake. The woman with the lilting voice had referred to the title of a book of short stories by Monsieur Raymond Carver.

Even so, for a few moments I'd thought the expression was meant for me. That misunderstanding would leave a mark on my psyche; it's what happens when you're a kid brother.

2

A Broken Window

THE IDEA OF BECOMING a reader on demand had been in my mind even before I moved to Quebec City.

I was born in a village in the Eastern Townships, where my father had a general store. My mother ran the household as well as waiting on women customers who came to buy lingerie. Now that she's no longer there I would like to describe her with a single word: she was protective. I mean, she was always watching over us, protecting us.

Aside from my brother Théo, whom we hadn't heard from for a long time, there were three children in the family: Jack, my little sister and me. When I say "little sister" it's just a manner of speaking; actually, she's a bit older than I am.

Jack was the first to leave home. He dreamed of being a writer and decided to move to the provincial capital. Then my sister left, saying that she wanted "to have a change of air and see the country."

My father stood six feet two. Slim, always nicely turned out, he had brushed-back hair and a fine moustache. According to Jack, he resembled the movie star Errol Flynn. In my eyes, he could do anything. I saw him expand the store and our house as well; he also built the counters, shelves and furniture, and he made a playground.

My memory of him is of a kind and sensitive man, but who had a temper violent enough to scare me. To placate him I always tried to be helpful. For instance, I would offer to "open up" on days when he felt like sleeping in.

First, I would take the broom and sweep up the dust and peanut shells left by customers the day before. After that, I stocked the shelves. I would go to the shed adjoining the store to get canned goods and other products: Aylmer soups, Carnation milk, Ideal peas, Old City honey, Salada tea, Fry's cocoa, Magic baking powder, Raymond pickles, and more. When I stacked the cans on the shelves I made it a point of honour to place them with the labels out and to line them up flawlessly.

Once that job was done I would turn on the radio to listen to the old songs my parents liked. It stood in a corner of the store that we called "the mill's window," as in the song. That was where my mother would sit in front of her Singer machine to do her sewing and mending. The light was good there because the window looked out on the yard where we liked to play cowboys and indians with the children next door.

If my head is still full of songs today, it's because of the radio that I listened to in the morning while I waited for my father. Songwriters like Leclerc, Brassens, Ferré and Barbara, singers like Catherine Sauvage, Juliette Greco, Cora Vaucaire, Yves Montand and Édith Piaf: that was what I listened to back then and the songs were etched onto my heart.

When I heard footsteps on the stairs I turned down the radio. I hoped with all my might that my father would see that I'd done a good job. In my opinion it was impossible not to see how carefully I'd swept up and filled the shelves.

But every time, I was disappointed. He didn't notice a thing.

In his defence I admit he had a lot on his mind. Running a general store was no picnic. You had to offer customers all sorts of merchandise: clothes and shoes, hardware, medicine, bulk food, floor covering, cans of paint, cigarettes, leaf tobacco.

In the shed, we kept fifty- and hundred-pound bags of white sugar, brown sugar, flour, beans, and pig-feed for farmers. We also had barrels of nails and salt pork.

In the cellar, perched on beams, were barrels and casks of molasses, coal oil, vinegar, as well as sheets of glass to be cut to measure. It was damp there and poorly lit and there'd been a constant strong smell, at once rank and sugary, since the day when, in a moment of distraction, I'd been slow to shut off the spout that let the thick molasses pour into a customer's jug.

The cellar was also where I did muscle-building exercises. I was as thin as a rail. The neighbourhood kids would beat me up in the schoolyard. In the winter, when we played hockey on the frozen river, they skated faster than I did. That was why I'd made myself a dumbbell from a broomstick stuck into a small maple log at either end. I could just barely lift it to the level of my chest and then above my head, like in the illustrations in the *Petit Larousse*. After each session I was sure I'd developed my biceps, broadened my shoulders and my chest. Soon I would be strong enough to carry the heavy sacks of grain piled up in the shed.

Unfortunately, our business went into a decline. My father, eaten up with worry, suffered a serious heart attack. He sold the store. My parents moved to Quebec City, to the St. Francis of Assisi parish where rents weren't too high. I moved in with them. After a few weeks, having found no job, I got the idea of placing an ad in the

Journal de Québec to offer my services as a Reader on Demand. I liked the French term, Lecteur sur demande, because of its initials—LSD. For me, reading is a drug.

There were more replies than I'd expected. I moved out of the family apartment and took a small apartment in la Tour du Faubourg in the Upper Town, where my brother lived.

Jack lives on the top floor, the twelfth, and I'm on the first. That's normal, he's a writer. He has an unbroken view of Lower Town and the Laurentian mountains.

Caught up in his work as he is, he doesn't often invite me to his place. I have the feeling though that he would be lost without me. He calls at any hour, asking me to root around in my memories. We always call him "old Jack." In fact he's not that old, but he has holes in his memory. He's quite capable of calling in the middle of the night because he's trying to think of a word and he can't get to sleep.

Once, he called at two a.m. to ask me if I remembered the "exact words" our father had used when we broke the glass in the door to the shed when we were playing hockey in the store.

3

The Death of Montcalm

Ten minutes to eight.

I was early. To get the lay of the land I drove very slowly past the house of the woman with the lilting voice. Then I parked the Mini Cooper on the street that runs along Jeanne-d'Arc Park and waited until it was time. Gardeners had planted the flower beds. It was early May and still light out.

At the appointed hour I got out of the car and headed for rue de Bernières. In my briefcase were the Carver stories and, just in case, two more books of his. This time I looked more closely at the house. It was brick and had three storeys; the top one, which had a dormer window, seemed to be an attic.

In the entrance there were two mailboxes marked with the numbers 1 and 2. The woman hadn't told me that the house was home to other people. After a moment's hesitation I punched in the door code. The door to upstairs opened and I was facing a staircase on my right and an apartment on my left. According to a plaque on the door frame, it was occupied by an architect. I started up the stairs.

When I got to the landing my heart began to beat faster. In front of me was an apartment with its door ajar. I gave a little cough to announce my presence. No sound from inside. There was a button for a doorbell, but it was covered with a strip of tape. I knocked three times on the doorframe. Three brief knocks but they sounded very loud. I had the feeling that all the people in the house had heard me and everyone had their ears pricked to listen to what would come next.

There was no movement in the apartment. I set down my briefcase and sat on the stairs. The woman had probably gone out on some last-minute errand. Why had she left the door open? To invite me to come in and wait for her? No, she'd have left a note.

My watch showed a quarter past eight. I decided to wait a few minutes, but outside rather than in front of an open door, like an intruder or a thief. Before I left I knocked three times again—a little louder than the first time. Still no answer, so I picked up my briefcase and left.

My head was full of questions as I sat on a bench on the edge of the Plains of Abraham. Keeping an eye on the front door, I took the Carver book out of my briefcase and started to read the story the woman had mentioned. To warm up I read aloud, always trying to place the emphasis in the right places, to keep a constant rhythm, and not to spoil the liaisons between words. I'm obsessive. Every ten seconds I glanced at the house.

The woman still wasn't back.

The day was fading and the light wasn't so good. I closed the book. As I always do when I'm hesitating over a course of action, I asked myself what my brother Jack would have done in my place. His determination set an example for me.

On the phone he'd explained that he was working very hard on a novel, the theme of which was the place of French in North America. He had done a thorough study of the defeat on the Plains of Abraham. The battle, which had lasted only half an hour, had been fought a few metres behind me. The Marquis de Montcalm had been killed, Canada had become a British country, and since then we all had death in our souls: that was how my brother put it.

Ten to nine. The more time passed, the more it was becoming obvious that the woman hadn't gone out on an errand. She'd had an accident, she'd fallen down and now was stretched out on the ground, unconscious. Immediately, I went back to the house and climbed the stairs. This time, I went into the apartment.

A big living room. No one there. The first thing I noticed was the mess. Books lying around on a coffee table, a sofa, even on the rug. Most were open. Oddly enough I could only see dictionaries and encyclopedias. On the bookshelves I recognized the six red volumes of the *Grand Robert de la langue française.*

All at once I realized that I hadn't even asked if anyone was there. I hastened to do so, in a quavery voice that I didn't like. No answer. Unable to dismiss the image of the woman lying on the ground, I walked to the hallway.

On the right was a wide-open door: the kitchen. With the aroma of real coffee. There was some in a barely touched cup on the table. Farther down the hallway, I saw two other doors, both shut. Pushing open the first took me into a bathroom. I held my breath because of the image in my head. But I was wrong, it was empty.

The last door opened onto a bedroom. I stood on the threshold, ready to run away at the slightest sound from the entrance or from the apartment below. A lace curtain covered the window. A dressing gown lay on the foot of the bed. There were dried flowers, and the scent of lavender filled the air.

No one was there but I felt I was committing an in-discretion so I beat a retreat and left the house as fast as I could.

As I was leaving my parking space I saw in the rear-view mirror that the old Mini Cooper was leaving streaks of rust on the road. The woman's absence had saddened me. Back home I hoped that there would be a phone message, but there wasn't.

4

Limoilou and the Red Pony

THAT SATURDAY I WENT to the Île d'Orléans as usual. I was going to read to Limoilou, a young girl who was convalescing. She lived in a chalet with a friend of my brother's named Marine.

Life is complicated. Although Marine is my age I'm not the one she loves: she is in love with my brother Jack. Given her Irish background, she has a wonderful mop of red hair, green eyes and a hot temper; you have to be serious when you talk to her.

Marine and my brother have taken Limoilou under their wing. Actually, it's Marine who takes care of her: Jack is writing his novel; he lives in another world.

On my way to the chalet I recalled some advice of Marine's from my first visit. When you drive off the bridge to the island, you climb the big hill and turn left. Don't drive too fast if you want to catch sight of Félix Leclerc's barn and the sign that shows the singer-song-writer from the back, hunched over his guitar. Three kilometres along you take a small dirt road that starts going gently down. Step on the brakes anyway and take the time to look at the flowers growing along the edge of the cultivated fields. You will drive past a lone birch tree that acts as a stopping point for the birds, like the hotels that welcome travellers. In the place where the hill becomes steep there is a trembling aspen with leaves that stir at the slightest breeze, with a sound like crumpling paper. After that the hill is even steeper and you see a chalet in a maple grove and beside it, the pond and the dock on piles.

I parked behind Marine's Jeep. The two girls were walking around the pond with the cats: the little black one and the old one called Chaloupe because of her big belly that sways back and forth like a boat.

Marine waved, then sat at the end of the dock. Limoilou came to join me, followed by the black cat with his tail in the air when he runs. She had on a long flowered dress and she was walking barefoot in the grass. When she held out her hand I pretended not to see the scar on her wrist.

Limoilou was a little better, physically anyway. In the winter, she and Marine had skated on the pond and sometimes skied the trails near the chalet. She had recovered her strength. As for me, I'd been reading to her since the spring, ever since the snow on the dirt road had melted. When it became impassable because of the mud, Marine would come to get me in her Jeep. She accorded great importance to my visits. Once, a bit carried away, she had said that reading sessions were a kind of therapy.

The young girl picked up the black cat in her arms and pushed open the door; I followed her inside. I was a professional reader and not just a little brother, so there was no question of emotion or nerves. In the solarium I set my briefcase on Marine's work table, which was covered with French-English dictionaries. My brother's friend worked as a translator; she was finishing the English version of his latest novel.

Limoilou settled onto a chaise longue. The black cat had run to the kitchen and you could hear her crunching her kibble. The girl was silent, as usual. She'd said bonjour as she shook my hand and that was all. I took my book and sat in a rocking chair and waited for the cat to come back. When he climbed onto Limoilou's stomach, I started to read. Between her and me it was a kind of ritual or something like that.

I was reading her *The Red Pony* by Monsieur John Steinbeck. The book told the story of a little boy, shy and polite, called Jody, who lived with his parents on a ranch in California. His father had given him a pony as a gift. Jody was trying now to break him, with the help of Billy Buck, a stable hand.

I was the one who had chosen that novel, because Limoilou hadn't expressed a preference. My choice rested on the fact that she enjoyed the company of horses: I'd had a chance to note that on my first visit. That day, showing me around, the girls had led me onto a winding path strewn with big stones that started behind the chalet and allowed you to go down the cliff. At the bottom we came out onto several fields separated by rows of loosestrife. One field, surrounded by an electric fence, served as grazing land for a group of old racehorses. Limoilou slipped in between the two wires. She stroked the muzzles of the horses, gave them berries to eat from her hand. According to Marine, she spent time telling them about the miserable years she had survived during her brief existence.

In Steinbeck's book, young Jody didn't have an easy time of it either. As the author said, "His father was strict about discipline. Before he left for school the ten-year-old had to feed the chickens and the cattle, fill the wood box and look after the pony, that is to curry him, brush him, braid his mane and start breaking him in."

While I read the story, which was full of concrete

details, I tried to see Limoilou's reactions. Her fingers were stroking the black cat under its chin. With her very short hair, the dark circles under her eyes, her narrow, delicate feet and the little blue vein that was throbbing at her left temple, she was at the same time beautiful and moving.

With half-closed eyes she was looking vaguely outside, in Marine's direction. All girls intimidate me, and I wouldn't have been able to read to her in a professional voice if her face had been turned towards me. Another thing, in my story the pony caught cold after spending a night in the rain; matters would take a turn for the worse and I didn't know how Limoilou would react.

When I was little, a cleaning lady would come now and then to give my mother a hand with the housework. Her name was Marie-Ange. In the kitchen after supper she would tell us old, old stories about Ti-Jean and the Giants. Those stories were very scary. Now I know that they also gave me courage and helped show me how to live.

5

The Four Simones

My love of reading goes back a long way.

The year when my father decided to enlarge the house he'd built two bookcases, one at either end of a solarium flooded with sunlight that stretched above the store. But we mainly had magazines such as *Life*, *Paris-Match*, and *Reader's Digest*.

Real books I would discover later, when I worked as the assistant to an uncle who travelled his rounds in a bookmobile. He was a character everyone called The Chauffeur. He had devised the plan to bring reading matter to people in far-flung areas who didn't have access to a municipal library.

His vehicle was an old milk truck that he'd converted with his own two hands. The shelves were tilted back slightly to keep the books from falling if they shifted. And because they were on rails, it was easy to have access to the kitchenette or the Murphy bed. The bookmobile was also a camper.

My uncle needed an assistant because he was about to start his longest tour of the summer. He was on his way to Charlevoix County and the North Shore, then he crossed the Saint Lawrence at Sept-Îles and kept on driving around the Gaspé Peninsula.

When we came to a village, the Chauffeur would set up the bookmobile in the most conspicuous spot: in front of the church or on the town wharf. I opened the two back doors and unfolded the running board. If readers were taking their time, I had permission to hang out in the area. Sometimes I would take a Tintin and read it by the riverside. Other books didn't appeal to me, except for the ones that talked about sports. I was fifteen years old.

One day when we were talking about what we were reading, the Chauffeur drew my attention to a small section devoted to sports. It wasn't hockey season but I chose a book about Henri Richard and took it to the beach.

Henri Richard was a kid brother like me. When he launched his career with the Montreal Canadiens, the team had been dominated for a long time by his brother, Maurice. Maurice broke records and his feats were legendary. One story claimed that he had scored a goal by dragging an opponent on his back. And one day when he'd worn himself out moving furniture, he had scored five goals and was credited with three assists even though he'd warned his team mates: "Guys, don't expect a lot from me tonight."

Without intending to, Maurice Richard had become a French-Canadian idol, saviour of the nation who would avenge the defeat on the Plains of Abraham. I only knew about his amazing feats through my father's stories and through black-and-white documentaries. But I didn't need much more to see that young Henri didn't have a hope of matching the accomplishments of his illustrious brother. He was in the same situation as I was in relation to Jack.

According to my book, Henri Richard was shorter and lighter than Maurice. He didn't speak English and in the locker room he didn't say a word. On the ice, though, he was swift. He had his own style: he would score a lot of goals while leaning with all his weight on the opponent trying to check him. His successes warmed my heart and at times I had the impression I was becoming an adult thanks to him.

For a long time I was only interested in sports. My work on the bookmobile, however, led me to a discovery. Observing readers, women for the most part, I saw that their behaviour was quite out of the ordinary. I am thinking in particular of a woman called Simone.

For two days now we'd been at Rivière-au-Tonnerre, on the North Shore of the Saint Lawrence. The Chauffeur had parked the bookmobile at the entrance to the wharf. The weather was steady and mild, and in the dry air, we could see far away. My uncle suggested we have supper in Havre-Saint-Pierre, the village that at the time marked the end of the road. But he kept putting off his departure: Simone hadn't come yet.

The Chauffeur kept looking at his watch. To pass the time he went down to the shore, pulled off his shoes, and took a few steps in the sand. I observed him from my seat at the back of the bookmobile where I sat with legs dangling. Usually it was the opposite: he would stay in the vehicle and I would go walking along the water's edge. On that day though, I wanted to leave as soon as possible because I was curious to see that "end of the road."

At last Simone appeared on her bike, skirt pulled up, knees throwing off sparks with every turn of the pedal. She said hello and apologized for being late. My uncle had told me two things about her: her first name came from three women her mother admired: Simone de Beauvoir, Simone Signoret and Simone Chartrand. And she was so beautiful that once you'd seen her you couldn't forget her.

Her bike was a pink CCM with balloon tires and a basket hooked onto the handlebars. From the basket she took a pile of books and put them in my arms. The Chauffeur came running, puffing, his shoes still in his hand. He gave her his arm to help her into the bookmobile. Then neither of us could take our eyes off her.

She moved slowly along the shelves. At first she didn't touch them, only looked, hands behind her back. Now and then she'd kneel down with one knee on the ground to study the lower shelves, and I stopped breathing because of her short skirt.

A moment later, she stopped in front of a book. She stroked the spine with her finger, cocked her head to one side to read the title, then picked it up. And I swear, while she was reading the first page there was a gleam in her eyes. A real one, not the beam of light they show in sci-fi films. Her whole face lit up.

Later, on our way home, I associated this with the sun flooding the solarium at our country place, where I settled in to read. From then on, to see that light again, I read all the books that came to hand.

6

Like a Thief

I WOKE WITH A START. It was five a.m. I had dreamed about the mysterious woman on rue de Bernières.

In my dream, it was dawn. The woman was leaving her apartment showing no concern for the scattered books or for closing the door. She had on a long muslin dress with a hood that was pulled up. I saw her from the back, descending the stairs like a ghost. No part of her could be seen, neither her feet nor her hands nor the rest of her body.

The woman arrived at the Plains of Abraham.

Patches of fog were scattering in the first rays of sunlight. You could make out soldiers covered in blood, lying in the grass, waving their arms to get help. She walked among the wounded without seeing them and appeared indifferent to their suffering. A few moments later she stepped onto a path that went down the cliff. At the Anse au Foulon she got into a small boat, then a big sailboat that was flying the fleur-de-lys flag.

My dream froze on one final image: the woman was in the prow of the sailboat that was rounding the headland of the Île d'Orléans, heading for the Gulf and old Europe.

Spellbound by that vision, I couldn't get back to sleep. I sat up in my bed. I could still hear the groans of the wounded but it was just the wind that was wheezing at my bedroom window. I got up and gulped down a bowl of cornflakes with strawberries I'd thawed the night before. After that I made coffee, but instead of drinking it, I wrote two phrases on a scrap of paper and slipped them into a pocket of my windbreaker. Then I went down to the basement and drove away in the Mini Cooper.

This time I parked near the Musée des Beaux-Arts. Very slowly, I walked back up rue de Bernières. There was fog over the Plains of Abraham, but nothing compared to what I had seen in my dream. I met two joggers running side by side.

I was nearly certain that the woman, after a longer than usual absence, had gone back home. The note I'd written and intended to slip under her door said quite simply:

Dear Madame,
I did not have the pleasure of making your acquain-

tance the day before yesterday when I came to your
house at the appointed time. If you would still like
a reading session, please call me.

Francis

Because of the early hour I wasn't surprised not to
hear even one sound in the house. Climbing the stairs I
tried to avoid any stair that creaked. On the landing I was
stunned to note that the apartment door was still ajar.

I was taken aback. The only thing that came to mind
was a song, the one that said: "Do not forsake me oh my
darlin'" which keeps coming back hauntingly in the film
High Noon. I was worried and a little sad. How was it possible for an apartment to be left open for nearly two days
with no one noticing? Had the woman been abducted?
Should the police be informed?

Having no answer to these questions, I went in without knocking. I removed my sandals so I wouldn't waken
the downstairs neighbour and took a few steps in the living room. Nothing had changed. The same mess. Books
all over, nothing but dictionaries and encyclopedias. As
I was less worked up than last time, it struck me as odd
that a person interested in Carver's short stories had no
literature in her library.

In the kitchen, I found the cup of coffee on the table.

In the bedroom, the dressing gown was still on the foot of the bed, and the scent of lavender still filled the room.

When I walked into the bathroom, to which I'd given just a quick look the first time, I saw there was a map on the wall behind the door. Approaching it, I noted that it was a street map of Paris. I'd seen one before when I was leafing through my *Petit Larousse*.

At the bottom of the map, fastened to it with thumb-tacks, I noticed a newspaper clipping. I ran my eyes over it. It was a clipping from *Le Monde* with the headline "French Thinking." The author of the piece pointed out that the map of Paris, split into two distinct parts by the Seine, reproduced quite faithfully the two hemispheres of the human brain.

On the rim of the tub and on a shelf above the water taps was a series of little jars, flasks, and vials of different shapes and colours. From them came a perfume I hadn't smelled during my first visit. Suddenly a very old memory came back to me.

Lying on my parents' bed with my head in my hands, I was watching my mother. I was probably around five years old. She was sitting at her dressing table and she had on a white outfit with straps that left her arms bare. Staring into a three-panelled mirror, she was powdering her cheeks, putting on lipstick and perfume. The heady

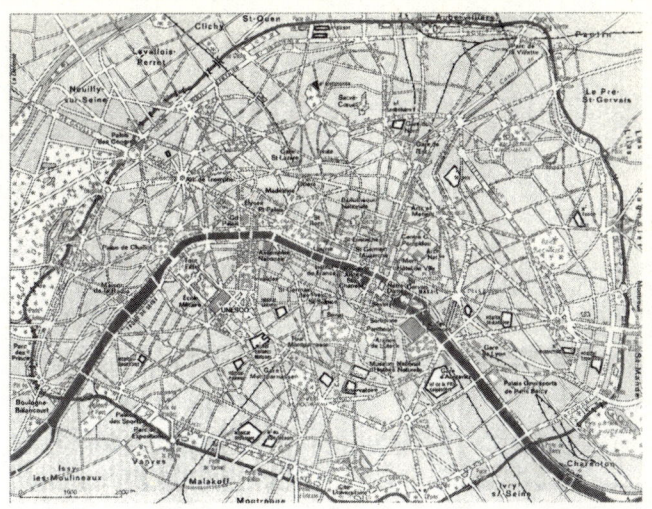

scent that filled the room was intoxicating, My mother was very beautiful and I wouldn't have given up my place for anything.

7

Fraying Clouds

MY BROTHER JACK is a workaholic. He is making progress with his novel and it is gradually taking over his life.

From high up in the Tour de Faubourg, he calls me more and more often, to refresh his memory. For instance, he forgets the dates of the main events that mark the history of Canada and the United States. I draw up lists and tables he can tape to the walls of his apartment.

At night when he is falling asleep, he can't help thinking about the last sentence he left incomplete, and all at once the words are there. He gets up, grumbling. To keep from waking altogether, he doesn't turn on a light. He gropes his way to the kitchen table, careful not to trip over the vacuum cleaner that always sits in the corridor. Sit-ting on the edge of a chair he jots something on a scrap of paper or on the back of an envelope. Then goes back to bed.

There are times when no sooner has his head hit the

pillow than the words come back, in complete sentences. An opportunity like that doesn't come often and he has to take advantage of it. So he gets up, switches on his desk lamp, and spends the night working.

It was on the telephone one Saturday morning that Jack was telling me about the woes of his trade. In the same breath, he asked me to drive him to Île d'Orléans. He hadn't seen Marine and Limoilou for three weeks. I agreed because, in any case, I had to go there myself and read to Limoilou. On that matter, he wanted to lend me a book he'd used for his novel, and he recommended that I read excerpts to his young protégée. It was from a book by Lewis and Clark entitled *Far West* that our sister had given him when he came back from a trip. The present was accompanied by a postcard on which she had written: "My heart goes with you on the roads of French America."

Jack was quoting that remark. It made me jealous because I was very attached to the person I always called "Little Sister." So as not to let it show, I asked my brother to tell me what Lewis and Clark had said. I knew nothing of the two men except that they were explorers and had reached the Pacific at a time when very little was known about the vast and empty spaces of the American West.

Jack did me the favour of not drowning me in a flood of information, pointing out just three facts: the

Lewis and Clark expedition as envisoned by President Jefferson had been carried out between 1804 and 1806. Its goal was to discover a river that flowed into the Pacific. It had started just after the Louisiana Purchase ceded that territory to the United States.

When he uttered the word "Louisiana", my brother spread his arms. We were driving along the super highway, not far from the ramp that leads to the island. As the morning was warm we had rolled down the windows of the Mini Cooper. Jack's right arm was hanging out the window and his left hand, waving around in front of my face, was blocking my view. Just as I was about to drive onto the bridge I had to make a hard right to avoid a truck coming in the opposite direction. My brother didn't notice a thing. I had never seen him so worked-up. He was waving his arms around and explaining to me that in the 18th century, Louisiana covered nearly half of the American territory, from the Great Lakes to the Gulf of Mexico, and from the Mississippi to the Rockies.

That vast region belonged to France. It had been explored by people I knew—Marquette and Jolliet, then the Cavalier de la Salle, and by others unknown to me, such as Henri de Tonty and Louis Hellepin. To avoid a longer list, I asked my brother if he really thought the book by Lewis and Clark could interest young Limoilou.

He stopped waving his arms and crossed them over his chest.

"I'll answer you," he said, "but I've got a couple more things to tell you."

"Go for it."

"When the French landed in America it was not enough for them to build fortifications to protect themselves from the cold and the Iroquois. They learned native languages. For the fur trade, they traveled by canoe and married Indian women. Most of all, they explored the country, crossed it in every direction. What I'm saying is they loved adventure. They loved freedom."

At that word, which made the first bars of a song by Georges Moustaki ring out in my head, my brother fell silent. I guessed that he was no longer there, that he was back in his novel. Out of respect I kept quiet too. Then, as we were approaching the dirt road, I reminded him gently that he hadn't answered my question.

"I'm sorry," he said. "The last time I went to the chalet I talked about my novel with Marine. Young Limoilou was there and she asked tons of questions about the Indians and the French. You'll see, they play an important part in the story of Lewis and Clark. Actually, it's a travel diary, I forgot to mention that."

It wasn't the only thing he had forgotten. I didn't

mention it because I'm a kid brother, but he ignored the fact that I always prepared for my reading sessions with the greatest care. I was a professional reader. There was no question of my turning up at someone's home without having acquired a good command of the text.

We had arrived. Jack rummaged in a grocery bag that held his possessions and took out two books.

"I didn't tell you that the journal is in two volumes: one for the trip there and one for the return."

"That's okay," I muttered.

Marine and Limoilou were inside. They were watching us through the big kitchen window. Before joining them my brother added that he'd put a map of Louisiana in with his belongings so that Limoilou could trace the route the explorers had taken.

I stayed in the car by myself. Choking back my bad mood, I opened the first volume. The cover showed a Sioux in war regalia, wielding a tomahawk. I rested the book against the bottom of the steering wheel and skimmed the preface, trying to learn as much as possible about how they got ready for the expedition. Then I started to read the journal. I read out loud, trying to bring out the tone of the words and the rhythm of the sentences. At the same time I was looking for passages that might stir Limoilou's interest.

Now and then I raised my head to see if my tardiness had them worried. I was making progress in my reading. I'd underlined several paragraphs and was quite proud of myself. All at once Jack and Marine came out of the house without looking at me. My brother had a dark blue sleeping bag under his arm. With old Chaloupe in the lead, they came down the narrow path lined with flowers surrounding the pond.

I was about to start reading again when I noticed that Limoilou was watching me behind the screen door in the solarium porch.

She was waiting for me.

I closed the book with my finger on the page I intended to start with. The first thing I noticed in the chalet was the map of Louisiana that my brother had put up near the door next to the kitchen. It was impressive.

When we were settled comfortably, she in her chaise longue and me in my rocker, I waited a few moments to respect our ritual: meditation, eyes closed, black cat on her belly. This time though, she declared in a determined voice:

"I'm ready!"

Enunciating carefully, I read the beginning of the journals:

I determined to go as far as St. Charles a french Village 7 Leag. up the Missourie, and wait at that place untill Cap. Lewis could finish the business he was obliged to attend to at St. Louis.

I Set out at 4 o'clock p.m., in the presence of many of the neighbouring inhabitents, and proceeded on under a jentle brease up the Missourie to the upper Point of the 1ˢᵗ Island. A heavy rain this afternoon.

I paused.

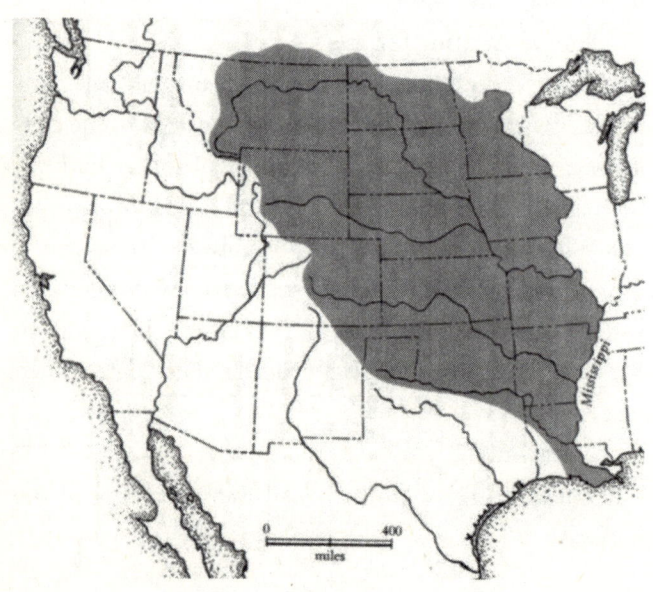

It was always the same when I was starting a new story: I wondered what effect the words would have. Sometimes they built bridges, other times a wall. You never knew.

Limoilou was fidgeting on her chair.

"In your story," she said, "there's a person who narrates it. Can you tell me who that is?"

"It's Captain Clark."

"That's right, there are two explorers, Lewis and Clark. Your brother Jack told me when he was putting up the poster."

"What else did he tell you?"

"They're going up the Missouri and then to the Pacific and they're going to have all kinds of adventures, especially because of the French and the Indians."

"And did he tell you about a woman of the Shoshone tribe?"

"No."

"Her name is Bird Woman. I'm pretty sure you'll like her a lot."

"Will I?"

She smiled timidly. A little like the sun you glimpse for a second behind fraying clouds. It was the first time that she'd asked questions and that her face lit up. And then my reader's soul was lighter, and I worked well until the end of the session.

It was nearly noon. I wanted to drop in and say hello to Jack and Marine before I left. On my way to the pond I spotted them in the distance. They were buried in the sleeping bag and it was rolling over and over, travelling down the gentle slope that led to the confluence of the streams that we called "where murmurs meet." For the second time that day I was aware of a speck of jealousy entering my heart and that feeling cancelled out the well-being that my work had brought me.

The sun doesn't shine very long for kid brothers.

8

The Black Panther

My clientele was not limited to Limoilou. It was expanding more and more, I'm proud to say. As well, I gave readings on the radio, in schools, and to book clubs.

Sometimes I would read my brother's books because he refused to promote them. It was better, in his opinion, for the book to occupy the foreground with the author in the back, as far away as possible. He did not consider himself to be a public man and the thought of being recognized on the street horrified him. Not only did he not give interviews, he raged against writers who explained in the media the meaning of their texts, and who held forth on their children, their sexual orientation; and their recipes. He was very fond of Hemingway's final words to the Nobel Prize jury.

I have spoken too long for a writer. A writer should write what he has to say and not speak it. Again I thank you.

Jack was mule-headed and I didn't even try to make him understand that his attitude was a form of self-destruction. I struggled instead to contribute modestly to spreading the word about his books, either by reading them to someone or by "forgetting" them in public places.

One of my clients at the time was a sick child. I would go to see him at the Laval hospital where he was waiting for an operation that would correct a cardiac malformation. He was twelve years old. It was his mother who'd found my ad in the *Journal de Québec*.

Reading to him required some precautions. As a valve in his heart did not function properly, doctors wanted to avoid his being infected by germs. Like the doctors and nurses, I had to wear a cotton mask, a long green smock and paper slippers. His name was Alexandre, but everyone called him Alex, which better suited his small stature. He was all by himself in a room. His mother had decorated the walls with drawings by his brothers and sisters. A teddy bear missing one eye sat on a window-sill.

When I entered the room I choked up. Electrodes were fixed to the child's chest and his wrists. Above his head was a screen that let you follow the beating of his heart. The device gave off a kind of sizzling sound that I forgot as soon as I started to read.

I was reading *Le tigre et sa panthère,* a novel from the French series Signes de piste I'd discovered in my uncle's library when I was little. The author was Monsieur Guy de Larigaudie. His book told the story of a young scout, whose totem is "the Tiger," who had embarked upon a voyage to India and the Far East. Following a shipwreck, he ends up on a deserted beach. Night is falling. He can hear the roar of a wild animal.

Looking up from my book I can see that the sick child has settled into his pillows and pulled the covers up to his neck. I look anxiously at the screen. As far as I can tell his heartbeat is normal, so I go on reading.

The Tiger thinks it's wise to sleep on the shore. He chooses a spot midway between the beginning of plant life and the tideline. For protection against any wild animals that might emerge from the jungle, he resorts to a ploy known to some adventurers. He looks for some long stalks of bamboo at the edge of the forest, then uses his scout's knife to shape one end to a very sharp point. One by one, he drives the posts into the sand, pointed end up, forming several concentric circles around him. Then he turns onto his side, digs a small hole for his hip and falls asleep under the stars.

The crackling of the apparatus has sped up, I raise my head for a second but there's nothing serious: young

Alex is now on his side too. He looks at me for a moment, then closes his eyes. Everything is normal.

In my story though, events are racing ahead. The scout is startled awake by a roar that tears into the night. He straightens up and grabs his knife, ready to sell his life dearly. In the moonlight he spies, very close to him, just at the periphery of the circles of bamboo, a wild animal writhing in pain. Leaping towards its prey, the animal has impaled its paws on the sharpened stalks. It's a black panther. She looks at him, fangs menacing, and there is anger in her golden eyes.

The door opens. The nurse enters, a mask covering the bottom of her face. The electrocardiograph is linked to the nursing station so she comes to see what's going on. I hadn't noticed that his heart was beating faster. Calmly and without a word, she studies the device, checks that the electrodes are in the right position. Then she straightens the pillows and, bending over the child, helps him turn onto his back while he drapes his arm around her neck. I can see on the screen that his heartbeat is faster at that moment. Mine would be too, I'm sure of it, if I were in his place.

Day is dawning over the beach.

The Tiger has moved away from the concentric circles and the panther. He walks on the edge of the sea and thinks things over. Suddenly he makes a decision. The scout walks into the jungle, finds a spring, and takes some cool water in a nut shell. The panther begins to growl when he approaches. She crouches, but her torn paws do not allow her to leap up. With slow movements and soothing words the scout sets down the water near her, then leaves. The panther starts to drink. Gradually she accepts his presence and he can tend her injuries.

The black panther allows herself to be tamed and I hope secretly that in the same way, my young client will be able to come to grip with his sickness.

9

The Garden Swing

ONE DAY DURING SUMMER holidays, my father suggested that I build a birdhouse. It had been raining since the day before and I was twiddling my thumbs.

My father went down to the cellar and I followed him without a word. The smell of molasses was stronger than usual because of the heat and humidity. He took a jig-saw, a hammer, some nails and half a sheet of plywood and set it all on the counter, leaning against the wall between two windows covered with spider webs. When I asked him if I should take my inspiration from a model, he advised me to choose the one that was somewhere inside my head.

First, I drew on the plywood the pieces that would become the floor and walls of the birdhouse. I cut them out, then nailed them together. Before I put up the front wall I made an opening for the birds to pass through. That's what I was trying to do when I saw through a window that it had stopped raining. My sister was outside, sitting in the big garden swing that had room for the whole family, or almost. I stopped working and joined her.

When I was sitting on the seat across from her she started talking about the countries she wanted to visit some day; she already knew the main ones because she was a fervent reader of our father's *National Geographic*. The air was mild, my sister was blinking her eyes in the sun, the back-and-forth movement of the swing kept telling me that the holidays would go on forever. That was all it took for me to forget the work that had been started in the cellar.

The next day it was my turn to open the store. When he came to take over, around half past nine, my father went down to the cellar without saying good morning and, needless to say, without a word about my cleaning and filling the shelves. A few seconds later he called me. Just from the way he said my name I could tell that I'd done something wrong. He was going to talk about the birdhouse.

Going down the stairs I could see at once that I was right. Planted in front of the counter, arms akimbo, he gestured to me to step up. In a firm but not aggressive voice, he announced that he was going to teach me something I'd be able to use for the rest of my life. And he declared: "When you start a job, son, you have to stick with it through to the end, till it's finished!"

That remark impressed me all the more because where work was concerned, I thought he was a champion. For instance, the summer when he'd enlarged our house, he had moved the "porch" practically on his own. In our house, that word meant a very broad shelter attached to the store and held up by two or three posts where farmers used to gather; I can still see him though, perched on the roof, using a simple handsaw to saw the beams that held the porch to the wall of the house.

When that hard work had been done, neighbours helped him move the shelter to the other side of the street. And then, working every day for several weeks, he'd been able to convert it into a garage big enough for his Buick, his Ford pick-up, and our three bicycles.

10

A 1992 Dodge Shadow

IMAGES OF MY FATHER doing some difficult task without complaining filled my head. They helped me keep going until whatever I was embarking on was done. The business of the mysterious woman though had left me with a feeling of failure. It seemed to me that I hadn't done my work properly.

To help me be clear in my own mind, I had to go back to rue de Bernières. I decided to go at dusk. During that brief hour when people turn on lights but don't close curtains, I had a chance of spotting the woman's silhouette. At the very least I would finally know if the apartment was inhabited.

As I'd done on my first visit, I left the Mini near Jeanne-d'Arc Park. To avoid looking like a peeping Tom, I took a detour through the Plains on my way to the house. I arrived at just the right moment, at dusk. Windows lit up one by one. Most people were finishing their supper or doing the dishes.

I slowed down. All at once I felt like taking my time. Maybe deep down, I would rather not be sure of anything. When I was fairly close to the house, I noticed there was a light in the apartment below: the architect was at home. In the loft, the skylight was very tiny and way too high. I couldn't see a thing. I studied the windows on the second floor, where the woman lived. Since I had visited the premises I knew to which room each one corresponded. Suddenly, at the big window in the living room, I thought I could see a shadow in silhouette. As if for two seconds, a person had leaned forward to look outside.

Maybe it was only an illusion so I went up to the black metal fence that lines rue de Bernières. Gazing intently at the window I spent ten or fifteen minutes trying to spot any sign of life.

In the neighbourhood nearly all the curtains were drawn. I waited another five minutes, then a minute more, and after that I went back to my car. I was overcome with doubt and dissatisfaction. Switching on the engine I started up without bothering to check that the road was clear. Suddenly, I realized someone was thumping on the hood of the Mini Cooper. I hit the brakes very hard. A little more and I'd run over him.

It was a man. Fortyish, taller than me, square-shouldered. He had on a grey fedora, a trench coat in beige or some pale colour. I watched him come around the car and approach the door. Leaning towards me he produced a badge but slid it back in his pocket before I had time to look at it.

"Turn off the engine!" he ordered.

I did. He walked behind the car, then opened the right-hand door and settled into the passenger seat.

"We're going to have a friendly conversation."

"Why?"

"Look over there!"

He pointed towards Jeanne-d'Arc Park. While I was turning my head in that direction he yanked out the ignition key. The move of a pro. Finally, I realized what this was all about: the man was a police officer. He had caught me observing the house on rue de Bernières. Now, that street is under the jurisdiction of the Plains of Abraham. Under the responsibility of the federal government, i.e. the Royal Canadian Mounted Police. Who I was dealing with then was one of the famous *police montée* as people used to say. The police who travelled on horseback in the big cities of western Canada, wearing a red tunic, baggy pants and a dented hat. The ones who were reputed to always catch their man.

A Mountie was sitting in the car beside me. I felt like

Henri Richard when his brother, Maurice, glared at him because he'd failed to score a goal.

"Don't be afraid," he said. "I'm not going to hurt you."

"I'm not afraid," I said, clearing my throat.

"Very good. Now then, explain to me what's so interesting about that house?"

"What house?" I said innocently.

He turned his head to me. With his impassive look and his metallic voice, he made me think of Humphrey Bogart. His fedora brushed the Mini's ceiling. To myself, I dubbed him "Bogie."

"The house on rue de Bernières," he said quite calmly. "The one you were gawking at for so long ."

"Is that against the law?"

"No, but it's not the first time you've come here."

I had to think. Fast. Someone, maybe a neighbour, seeing me go inside, had called the police. The house was under surveillance and Bogie was in charge of the investigation. He knew things about me. Having done nothing too serious, I did not really feel guilty. Rather, what I felt was irritation. I had constructed an imaginary world around the mysterious woman and now an intruder was entering my little universe at the risk of it all falling apart.

"You went to see a woman," said the cop. "What was the reason for your visit?"

"She'd invited me."

"Why?"

"To read to her."

"It's true. You're a professional reader."

"Yes."

So there, it was the right attitude: short truthful answers, and then wait. It was all good, and I was pleased with myself.

"She wasn't there but you went in anyway. Why?"

"The door was open."

"If you see an open door you walk in?"

"I was concerned."

"Why?"

"Maybe she had hurt herself. For example, while taking her bath."

"Oh yes! She was taking a bath with the door open!"

That was how to do it: answer succinctly, tell the truth, and wait for what would come next. All was well, I was fairly pleased with myself.

The policeman's sarcastic tone was getting on my nerves so I decided not to answer any more questions. Moments later, he stopped his interrogations. And most likely to show that I wasn't big enough to fight with him, he gave me a hint of what he knew about me. The number of times I'd come there. The places where I'd parked my car. My address in the Saint-Jean-Baptiste neigh-bourhood.

To finish, he made a proposal:

"You and me we're going to make a *deal.*"

"A what?"

"A *deal!* You don't know what a *deal* is?"

"You mean a *marché*?"

"That's it."

It was a fine opportunity to take my revenge. I was going to put this *police montée* in his place. Did Henri Richard, though small, not respond to every attack by his opponents on the ice?

"The two words are equivalent," I asserted. "They have exactly the same weight."

"So?"

"So, why did you use the English word?"

He shrugged. I was getting more and more angry and I was in no mood to hide it.

"I'll tell you why: it's because you think that English is a magic language."

Again, Bogie turned his head to observe me. His face was impassive, glacial even. He seemed to be asking himself if I was in my right mind. After thinking it over for a moment, he said, very calmly:

"During your second visit you took something from

the apartment. Here's my deal: you give me that object and in exchange, I'll tell you about the woman in question."

He put back the ignition key and opened the door.

"You've got a week to think it over. Good luck, Monsieur Francis!"

With those words he walked away. Before starting up I followed him with my eyes in the rear-view mirror. He wore big heavy shoes like all policemen. At the corner of rue Laurier he got into an old black car. I'm an expert on cars: it was a Dodge Shadow, probably a 1992.

11

The Masked Marvel

HENRI RICHARD CHARGED straight at the opposing team; he was unstoppable. Too bad, but I don't have his courage. When life creates problems, I sometimes indulge in dreams.

The day after my confrontation with Bogie, I gave in to my favourite dream. It involved a hockey game, back when goalies were starting to protect their faces with a mask. I am too young to have known those years but my father has talked to me about them. He told me how Jacques Plante, the Montreal Canadiens' goalie, had a fibreglass mask moulded to hug the contours of his face, with very small openings for eyes, nose, and mouth.

The best way to set off a waking dream is to lie in the fetal position. I lie on my left side, knees pulled up, one hand under the pillow, the other between my legs. Closing my eyes I empty my mind.

The first image arrives: we're at the Montreal Forum. Dressed in the goalie's uniform with the goalie's mask over my face, I jump onto the ice and into the light followed by all my teammates, with the captain last, according to tradition. Spectators, players—everyone thinks I'm Jacques Plante because I'm wearing his mask and because I mimic the way he skates. Meanwhile, the actual goalie is locked away in a small space next to the dressing room, under the surveillance of an equipment manager I'd been able to bribe.

I learned how to skate on the frozen river in my hometown village. When my father decided the ice was thick enough, we would clear a rectangular space by shovelling snow up the sides. Then I could skate with my sister or play hockey with the kids next door, where I was quite happy in the net.

At the Forum I make my way to the Canadiens' goal. With my blades I scrape the ice to roughen it in case I have to fall to the ground and pull myself back up speedily. I place my Sherwood stick on top of the net, then I take out a book I'd hidden inside my big mitt. My teammates zip around our zone. They don't look surprised that I've brought something to read. Everyone knows that Jacques Plante is a character.

I open my book. It is a collection of poems, *Les îles de la nuit*, by Monsieur Alain Grandbois. I don't always understand what I'm reading but the poems seem to increase my concentration and to sharpen my reflexes. Here are my favourite lines:

We have shared our shadows
More than our lights
We have shown ourselves
More glorious than our wounds
Than scattered victories
And happy mornings

Raising my head, I spot the referee who's been looking my way from centre ice. I gesture to tell him it's time to drop the puck. Our opponents are the Detroit Red Wings, with the daunting Gordie Howe. Luckily Jean Béliveau grabs the puck and with a few elegant strokes of his blades, as if it were a waltz, he skates into Red Wings territory. To help him, my favourite defenceman, Doug Harvey, advances towards the enemy blue line. My mind at rest, I go back to Grandbois's poems.

Ah, how our feeble fingers grope desperately
Trying to touch the tip of the world of dreams
Trying to rig out the caravel sailing towards
    miraculous isles.

A murmur rises among the spectators. Without letting go of my book, I can tell that our opponents are now in possession of the puck. From the corner of my eye I see Gordie Howe himself charging towards our zone along with two teammates. Before he crosses the blue line he shoots a pass to his centre. When he enters our territory, the people in the stands howl to warn me. I don't even look. Half-turned to the left, elbow on the cross bar of the net, I pretend to be absorbed in the poem. I look as if I couldn't care less about the encroaching danger, but I know that Gordie Howe is in the right-hand corner of the rink and that the centre has shot him the puck. I know him, he wants to draw our defenceman towards him and make a pass to his left winger who is stationed at the mouth of the net. Our forwards can't wait to lend a hand to the defencemen.

The crowd at the Forum are on their feet, yelling to make me react before it's too late. The clamour of the crowd fills me with pride, though I don't want it to show. I didn't go to school as long as my brother Jack, I haven't travelled as much as Little Sister, but to thousands of fans I'm the only person who can save the Montreal Canadiens.

I prolong the pleasure, savouring every second as it passes. Suddenly our defenceman, Doug Harvey, positions himself in front of Gordie Howe to check him. He is greeted with an elbow to his face. And then the great Gordie leaves the corner of the ice with the puck. The other defenceman, Butch Bouchard, blocks his way but the attacker delivers a perfect pass to his left winger who is nearly at my net. People hold their breath, in the stands there is a deathly silence.

Just when the left winger is about to drive the puck into the net, and as if nothing were going on I hold out my stick and just like that, I deflect the shot into the crowd.

I am the Masked Marvel.

12

The Indian Chiefs

My life was fluctuating between dream and reality. Far from worrying me, the situation was grounds for pride. I've never felt the need to be like everyone else.

In any case, my work as a reader gave me tremendous satisfaction. Every week I looked forward to seeing Marine and young Limoilou. Her mind was more and more alert and she asked lots of questions about the Indians. She had a weakness for the Sioux chief who appears on my copy of the Lewis and Clark journal.

At the last reading session I had left Clark all alone on a small island in the Missouri. The members of the expedition were resting from the first day of their journey. They had been warned that they would have to "cross a country held by savage peoples, many in number, powerful and warlike, fierce, treacherous, and cruel and in particular, enemies of the white man."

While the lovely Irish lass was carting her dictionaries into the kitchen, Limoilou settled into her chaise longue. She closed her eyes and I began reading. Because of the ordeals she had lived through, traces of which could still be seen around her eyes and on her wrists, she impressed me as much as ever. I was becoming bolder and at times I followed on her face the emotions that words provoked in her.

In his journal, William Clark noted that he had gone up the Missouri as far as the village of Saint-Charles, with some forty men who had set out on three boats. His comrade, Lewis, had finally joined him. They'd hired two Métis trappers, Pierre Cruzatte and François Labiche, who knew the area and who spoke several Indian languages.

Going back up the Missouri was difficult because of the currents, the sandbanks, and the tree trunks floating beneath the surface. If it were less windy, the men posted on shore would have been towing the big boat with cables. Limoilou's lovely face reflected the exertions by the members of the expedition, then it relaxed while they were preparing for the night because the authors remarked: "Ticks and mosquitoes are the worst pests." A sentence that always made him smile.

As for me, I was thrilled to note that the explorers' route is sprinkled with French names. Names of villages,

forts, waterways, hills—but also travellers, guides, adventurers, fur traders. Their names are Loisel, Dorion, Laliberté, Lepage... Their names sounded familiar and I uttered them with particular respect because they had been forgotten by history.

As Limoilou was particularly interested in the Indians, I skipped a long section of the diary to arrive at September 25. That was the day when the explorers encountered a band of Sioux famous for their ferocity. The Sioux controlled the passage to the Upper Missouri and demanded a ransom from the travellers. Their chief,

Tortohonga, was known as the Partisan. According to Pierre-Antoine Tabeau, he could on the same day "show himself to be faint-hearted and a firebrand, proud and servile, provocative and conciliator—a schemer and a hypocrite."

"What does 'firebrand' mean?" asked Limoilou.

Having anticipated the question, I'd consulted the dictionary before I left my apartment. I had no trouble then explaining that firebrand means literally a piece of burning wood with which to fire a cannon or, figuratively, a person who provoked squabbles.

"Thank you," she said. "How was the meeting with the Partisan?"

"Not great," I said.

And to illustrate my remark I read the next passage:

We invited the chiefs on board and showed them the air cannon and all the curious things that we knew would amuse them. We succeeded all too well for after we have given them the quarter of a glass of whisky (which they seemed to like very much) they drained the bottle and without delay became tiresome.

"The explorers shouldn't have given them whisky," Limoilou remarked, sensibly.

"You're right. It was an appalling habit. It had existed since the first meetings of Whites and Indians. But I suppose you learned all that in your history classes?"

She shrugged her shoulder and I saw a cloud pass over her sad and poignant face. I was sorry I had asked the question. Thank goodness, she asked if the authors talked about the women who were part of that Indian band. I hastened to read the paragraph to her:

The squaws are of an agreeable temperament (...)
They have high cheekbones, they wear skirts and
tunics made of skins, over their shoulders. They
do all the difficult tasks and I can assure you that
they are the absolute slaves of the men.

Limoilou was fidgeting a little on her chaise longue but made no remark so I went on reading.

The women then moved forward, dressed in bright
colours. Some held a stake from which hung an
enemy scalp, others held aloft rifles, lances, or var-
ious trophies brought back from the war by their
spouses, their brothers or their relations (...)

Their dances do not follow precise steps but slip and
slide and the music seems to be only a mixture of

slaps powerful or weak applied to the skin of their drums.

"Hang on a minute," she said. "Did you really say that the women danced, swishing an enemy scalp at the end a stick. Are you sure that's how it happened?"

She appeared tense, she looked worried. This time, having not anticipated the question, I thought it over as fast as I could. As I'd already gone over the writings of Champlain; those of Gabriel Sagard; the *Jesuit Relations*; and several other documents, I knew about the harsh treatments the Indians reserved for their enemies. They humiliated them, insulted, tortured, and in certain cases, devoured them.

How to explain such behaviour to a girl whose life had been devastated by physical and emotional suffering? I was racking my brains in search of a solution when I heard the sound of a chair being moved in the kitchen. A moment later, Marine came into the solarium and placed her dictionaries on the big table.

"I've finished my work," she declared.

It was the first time she had interrupted during a reading session. I understood right away that she did it to help me out. She moved from the window that was between me and Limoilou, and she began to stretch in the light that bathed the solarium. She arched her back

72

and stretched her arms above her head, holding her hands together with her palms up. It was eleven thirty in the morning and the sun burnished her magnificent red hair. I swear that her hair was on fire. Like me, Limoilou looked at the spectacle with eyes made huge with admiration.

"I'd like to go for a walk," said Marine. "Maybe I'll take the path that goes down to the park with the race-horses."

"That's a good idea, said Limoilou, "I'll come too."

They left the chalet together. The black cat, who had slept on the young girl's stomach, began to follow them. I didn't see Chaloupe but she couldn't have been very far.

I thought it over, then decided to withdraw on tip-toe. When they'd disappeared behind the chalet, I got into the Mini Cooper, closing the door without a sound. While the car was climbing the hill en route for the Chemin Royal, I remembered a very short quotation. I could have recited it to Limoilou by way of an answer her question. Those few words had the power and the delicacy to calm her worries. They had been spoken by the Grand Chief Crowfoot of the Blackfoot tribe:

"What is life?" It is the flash of a firefly in the night. It is the breath of a bison in winter. It is the small shadow that runs in the grass and is lost by sunset.

73

13

Marianne

ONE DAY, AROUND five o'clock, I was driving home in the Mini Cooper. My garage at the Tour du Faubourg, opens onto rue d'Aiguillon. As the door does not open automatically, I got out of the car to use my key when all of a sudden I noticed the old Dodge Shadow parked a short distance away. Bogie was at the wheel. I recognized him by his fedora and the turned-up collar of his trench coat.

Acting as if I hadn't seen him I inserted the key into the metal box. The door opened. Inside the garage, I took the ramp that led to the first basement. Getting out of the Mini I saw that the policeman had followed me on foot. Arms crossed, he was blocking my access to the concrete staircase that led to the upper levels.

"Bonjour, Francis!" he said, loudly enough to be heard over the deafening sound of the ventilators. "Remember me?"

The question struck me as idiotic. I didn't answer.

"Remember our … *deal*?"

"How am I supposed to forget that!"

"Very well, I'll walk you home, if you don't mind."

"What if I do mind?"

With a ceremonious wave of his hand, he motioned to me to take the stairs. When we were at the first floor he led the way to my apartment. It appeared that he wanted to show me that he knew exactly where I lived. I wasn't impressed because that information was on the list everyone could see in the front lobby on rue Saint-Jean.

Opening the door of the apartment I took the liberty of repeating the gesture with which he had made fun of me. He went inside and straight to the French window. Right next to it, on the left, was a tall, narrow chest of drawers where I kept my important papers. The address book I'd taken from the woman was in the top drawer.

"Your view's not as nice as Jack's," he observed.

Had he been bold enough to go up to my brother's apartment? Was he bluffing? I was inclined believe the second hypothesis but there was nothing to prove I was right. That Mounted Policeman was quite capable of turning up at Jack's apartment and sticking his badge under the man's nose for half a second. As a precaution, I pretended that I hadn't heard his remark.

This was not the time to disturb old Jack. For some mysterious reason he reckoned he had little time left to live. His novel about French America was to him a final combat. His battle on the Plains of Abraham. All his energy was devoted to his book. His backache was getting worse, he hardly ever went out, never went to a movie or ate out, and entertained no one. He was thin and wan.

My sister and I had the key to his apartment. She took care of his meals. Once or twice a day she opened the door without a sound and placed the hot dishes on the chair in the entrance. If Jack was working in his room she went on tiptoe, did some cleaning and tidying, washed the dishes, while I dealt with the messages accumulated on his answering machine. I had a look at his mail and paid the bills to spare him any trouble. Now and then we did a wash in the laundry room on the main floor. Weekends, I took him to the island to spend a few hours with Marine, Limoilou and the cats.

The policeman wandered through the apartment and nosed around in the corners. I was well aware that he was looking for the notebook but as he had complicated my life, I decided to make him wait.

"Do you know my brother's books?" I asked.

"I've heard about them," he said cautiously.

"Have you read them?"

"No, I'm not much of a reader."

"Not even detective novels?"

"I'd rather watch TV, it's more restful."

"That's too bad."

"Why do you say that?"

"TV only exists to sell things."

He stood still and gave me a look as if I'd come from outer space. In fact we lived in very different worlds. He must spend days at a time following people, spying on them with binoculars, eavesdropping on them in a restaurant or a hotel lobby behind a newspaper. Evenings, he was probably very happy to put on his slippers and sink into an easy chair, feet on a hassock, to watch whatever was on TV over a beer and pizza.

"What are you laughing at?"

"Nothing important."

"Let's get back to the reason for my visit. Where did you put the notebook? In the little chest of drawers?"

He hadn't waited long enough so I paused before saying anything. Also, I had just discovered something. On the wall to the right hung a painting by Jean-Paul Lemieux that showed a man, a woman, and a little boy. Because the painting was a reproduction under glass, I could use it for observing the policeman as if it were a mirror without his noticing anything. Looking at him like this, I was amazed to discover that he looked a lot like my father. He had the same gaunt face, the same serious and busy manner.

I tried hard not to show my surprise. But the only thing that came to mind to describe it was the English expression "poker-face." Why that expression instead of the French equivalent *visage impassible*? Had I too gone so far as to think that English was a magic language?

The policeman broke into my reflections.

"In the top drawer?" he insisted.

Right now I wanted him to leave and the sooner the better.

"That's right," I said, "the top drawer."

"Thanks. I knew it."

He took the article, leafed through it for a moment, then slipped it into the inside pocket of his trench coat. I stood with arms akimbo.

"Now that you've got the notebook would you kindly leave me alone?" I asked, speaking very deliberately.

"You don't want me to tell you about Marianne as we'd agreed?"

"About *who*?"

"The woman who lives on rue des Bernières. Didn't you know her name was Marianne?"

I nearly answered no, which was the truth. On the

phone she hadn't given her name and it didn't appear on the mailboxes. At the last moment I decided not to say anything.

"I couldn't care less about your information."

Then I pointed to the door.

After he'd left I tried to put some order in my ideas. It wasn't my strong point: generally I let myself be guided by instinct or feelings. This time again, my efforts gave no results.

At suppertime I fixed myself some spaghetti with meat sauce that my sister had brought. While I was doing the dishes, my hands in warm water and mind wandering, it occurred to me that I could not make any progress in my thinking unless I reconciled three elements: the map of Paris I'd seen in the bathroom; the strange dream that was set on the Plains of Abraham; and the name of the woman the policeman had just disclosed.

That day, though, it was impossible for me to go any further. After all, I'm just a kid brother.

14

The Big Hill at Baie-Saint-Paul

AMONG MY LISTENERS, the one to whom I was most attached aside from Limoilou was at the Hôtel-Dieu. Her name was Chloé. Her parents had called her that because of the character in *L'écume des jours* or *Froth on the Daze*, by Monsieur Boris Vian. She was twenty years old at the time of her stay in the hospital.

She was in a coma.

The accident had happened at the beginning of summer. Her boyfriend was driving a Yamaha and she was on the passenger seat, arms wrapped tightly around his hips. It was raining that day, and fairly cold. The bike had skidded on the big hill that fell away sharply on the way to Baie-Saint-Paul. The girl had been flung into the ditch and her head had struck a rock. She was not wearing a helmet.

Generally when I read to Chloé her boyfriend was there, holding her hand. He felt responsible for the serious injuries she'd suffered. On the day before the accident he'd taken the passenger helmet home to clean the plastic visor and forgot to put it back in the bike's carrier chest. Of course when he went to his friend's place to suggest a drive around Charlevoix, he had offered his own helmet. She'd just shrugged and said with a smile: "I trust you." Those few words echoed in his head when he woke up in the night.

I was reading her a novel by Monsieur Ducharme, *L'avalée des avalés* because it was on her course reading list. But there was another reason too. It seemed to me that words, in addition to possessing therapeutic virtues like plants, reacted with each other in the manner of atoms. That was very clear in Réjean Ducharme's writing: the words collided with one another, knocked together, so their power was multiplied tenfold. The first sentences hit me like a fist:

Everything swallows me. When my eyes are closed it's by my stomach that I'm swallowed, it's in my belly that I suffocate. When my eyes are open it is by what I can see that I'm swallowed, it's in the belly of what I can see that I suffocate. I am swallowed by the St. Lawrence River which is too wide, by the sky which is too high, by the flowers that are too fragile, by my mother's too-beautiful face.

The boyfriend was sitting beside the bed on a straight chair, stroking her hand. I stood, elbows leaning on the windowsill, to take advantage of the natural light. Lying on her back, Chloé appeared to be sleeping. She was on an IV and a monitor watched over her brain's activity, but she was breathing on her own.

I was in a new situation now. According to my *Petit Robert* dictionary the word *coma* means "deep sleep." In reality, the girl was lost in a strange country of which we knew practically nothing. We could only say that she existed somewhere between life and death, and that one day she would have to choose one world over the other. My job was to influence her choice. And to get there I had nothing but words.

Fortunately, Ducharme's writing was exactly the opposite of a "little music." It shuddered, it moved constantly, the words collided, the images went off in every direction, took on every colour, and bits of sentences sprang up like fireworks. I particularly liked the following passage:

> *Here, it is an island. It is a long road surrounded by rushes, arrowheads and showy small poplars. It is a long warship anchored just above the surface of the water on the edge of a river that runs to the sea. It is a large boat whose sides laden with*

iron and coal are nearly swallowed up, their single
mast is a dead elm tree.

The girl's friend and I were around the same age. I
would have given anything for him to find her again. I
assumed my gravest, most persuasive voice. I hoped with
all my heart the words would come to pierce the wall of
silence that surrounded her and that they would be able
to clear a path to that mysterious place where her soul
was curled up like a small animal deep inside a burrow.

There were times when I was overwhelmed by doubt.
I would regain confidence when I read these sentences
that it seemed had been written just for her.

I was so thoroughly walled in, I kept my valves
so tightly closed during those years of exile that
tonight, as on many other nights, I hit my head
on the floor the way you bang a watch that has
stopped against the corner of a table.

After that I said nothing. I kept an eye out for the
slightest sign of awakening. A quiet sigh, a blink, anything at all.

15

The Third Avenue Bridge

A sound attracted my attention when I was in the shower.

I turned off the taps and pricked up my ears. Someone was rapping on the door, using himself as a knocker. It seemed to me that the metallic sound was reverberating all the way to the end of the corridor. I dried myself off with three flicks of a towel and put on my old bathrobe. I went to the front door barefoot, after first looking through the spyhole. It was my sister, my beloved Little Sister. After knotting the belt of my bathrobe I quickly opened the door. Her face was tanned, hands behind her back, and a mysterious smile. Putting her arm around my waist and her nose on my neck, she said:

"Mmm—that smells good! What's in your shampoo?"

"Honey and lemon."

In spite of her long absences, my sister has always been my best friend. Important things, those that guide me through life I have learned from her or my father.

We share a ton of memories. One of the oldest goes back to the time when she was still living in the family house. When I opened the store she sometimes came and sat with me at the "window of the mill" and together we would listen to the famous songs that were played on the radio in the morning. As well, we sometimes leafed through one of the magazines my father subscribed to. Brushing shoulders and elbows, just enough to give us a little shiver, we would look at photos of the glamorous lives of the stars and celebrities of the day. One of those photos in *Paris-Match* would become for us the saddest in the world: it showed a grave freshly dug in the grass of a cemetery in Ketchum, Idaho, to receive the body of a man whom everyone in the world called Papa. It was Monsieur Ernest Hemingway. He had fired a bullet into his head on Sunday morning, July 2, 1961.

"Are you all right?" my sister worried.

"I could be. You?"

"Me too."

"You were at Jack's place?"

"Yes, but I didn't see him," she said. "His bedroom door was shut and I could hear snoring."

"Maybe he hadn't slept well. The last time I took him to the cottage he told me that he often got up in the night to write. He's afraid he won't get to the end of his novel so he's working even harder than usual."

"Anyway, I left him some croissants. I kept some for you and me too."

She held out a little bag she'd hidden behind her back.

"You're really an angel."

Leaning towards her I rubbed my nose against hers. This time she put her arms around my neck and her lips grazed mine. It was very sweet and gentle. In our relationship my sister and I rejected all rules but the one stipulating that neither of us imposed our will on the other. We did not need to go from thoughts to acts: it was enough for us to dream that everything was possible.

My sister left her sandals in the entrance. She went to the kitchen and put the croissants in the oven. I made coffee while she was setting the table with cutlery and several jars of jam. When we were sitting across from one another and eating, she put her bare feet on mine.

"Know what?" she asked.

That little question always heralded something special. I was on the alert.

"What?"

"Last night I walked along rue de Bernières."

"And?" I asked after taking a long sip of coffee.

"I was in luck. The woman was there."

"In her apartment?"

The reply didn't come right away. My sister was holding a bit of croissant, hesitating between strawberry jam and raspberry and bitter orange marmalade.

"No," she said, groping for words. "She was walking ahead of me on the sidewalk. She was going to get groceries. At least that's what I thought anyway."

"Why?"

"She had… she was holding a burlap bag to carry her groceries."

My sister's hesitations sowed seeds of doubt in my mind. Had she invented that story to make me happy? I kept my thoughts to myself because running through my head was the song *Fais comme si*, sung by Édith Piaf:

Act as if, my love,
Act as if we loved each other,
My love, my love
Just for a day, just for a day.

"Let me guess," I said. "The woman was walking ahead of you. To get a look at her face, you walked past her on some pretext or other."

"I had a stone in my sandal."

"Can you describe her?" I asked, uneasy.

"Sure," she said. "Tall, blonde. Very slim, pale complexion. Long white dress… Looked like a character in a Jean-Paul Lemieux painting."

Her index finger was pointing to the picture under glass that had let me observe Bogie surreptitiously. I stood up to have a closer look at the painting. As I got up from the table I could see through the French door that the sky was clouding over. My sister approached and I showed her the female figure that occupied the whole left side of the painting:

"Is this the woman you're talking about?"

"No, no, she's got on a grey-blue dress. I was thinking of that one."

She pointed to a small white silhouette in the middle of the canvas that measured just a few centimetres. I'd never noticed it. It seemed to be about to disappear on the horizon. I then had a brief *flash*—as people say who think English is a magic language. In a split second I realized the woman was disappearing from my life.

Who had she come for? Why did she leave? Kid

brothers can't answer questions like those. I simply had the impression that the part of me associated with my childhood was starting to come undone. That thought made me feel melancholy, and my sister was aware of it.

"Are you sad because of the story I told you?"

"No. I'm sad because I'm getting old. But it's not serious."

"What does it mean to you, getting old?"

"Becoming reasonable."

She looked me in the eyes for a long moment, then she stroked my cheek. Her hand was slow and warm and I wanted very much to know what would come next, but suddenly the grumbling of thunder could be heard.

A storm was brewing.

"I'd better go home," she said.

"How did you get here?"

"Bus."

"I'll drive you home in the Mini."

"You're incredibly nice."

The storm burst just as we were arriving at rue de la Couronne. The rain was pelting down, the wind was gusting and one could hardly see a thing. I slammed on the brakes, switched on the headlights and made the windshield wipers speed up. It took a few minutes to cross boulevard Charest, but after that all the traffic lights were green. I had no trouble getting to rue Prince-Édouard, where I turned right after I'd asked my passenger if the bus lane was empty.

My sister was staying with a girlfriend awaiting a divorce who lived in a two-bedroom apartment on 3rd Avenue. This time she had decided to stay in Quebec City until old Jacques had finished his novel.

"You're a very good driver," she said.

"I'm going to tell you a little story to say thanks."

"True or made up?" I asked.

"A true story. Do you know what Jack told me the last time I saw him?"

"What?"

"He talked about his novel on French America. Originally, he'd seen it as a kind of epic. The stories were all there in his head: Champlain and his plan for an alliance with the Indians; the explorers who expanded the territory all the way to the Rockies and to the Gulf of Mexico; the *coureurs de bois* and the adventurers who covered the regions in every direction; politicians from Louis-Joseph Papineau to René Lévesque, who protected the French language and institutions; the ordinary people, especially mothers, who ensured the country's survival through their daily labour."

She stopped to take a breath, then went on:

"All those people Jack wanted to include in his book. But when he started to write, the words came to him in bits and pieces and every day, the story lost its scope and its power. That's what he said. Finally, he told me it had been the same thing with all his books."

"Was he discouraged?"

"I don't know. He said: 'When you've been writing for a long time it's hard to remember clearly what's true and what's false. Some days you even wonder if you're alive or dead.'"

My sister gave me a sidelong glance. Unsettled, I couldn't think of anything to say. I reduced the speed of the windshield wipers because the rain had let up.

We were nearly at the Dorchester Bridge that spans the Saint-Charles River and leads to 3rd Avenue. The rain stopped. I switched off the wipers and automatically glanced in the rear-view mirror. We were being followed: the goddam Shadow was behind us. When I explained to my sister what was going on she turned around and admitted that she'd seen that car several times parked in front of her friend's apartment. We were in the middle of the bridge. She asked me to stop the Mini, just to see. I obeyed and right away the Shadow stopped too. Bogie got out of the car and went to lean against the parapet. As usual, he was wearing his fedora and his trench coat.

With his head tilted to one side he seemed to be looking at the water running towards the river.

She got out of the Mini slamming the door and headed for the man. I watched the scene in the rear-view mirror. The policeman was pretending not to see her.

"Hold on a sec," said my sister.

When she touched his shoulder he turned around. Then she started talking to him. She wagged her finger under his nose, her face very close to his, it was a genuine shouting match.

Abruptly, she left him and came back to me. Midway she stopped. She merely turned her head in his direction. I saw him rush into the Shadow. The black car made a U-turn at the entrance to the bridge and I lost sight of it when it drove onto rue Prince-Edouard.

I hoped I would never see it again.

16

An Attack of Depression

IF I WERE TO GO BY my own experience, the next book I would read to Limoilou would be something out of the ordinary. I even thought it could have an influence on the rest of her life. I had to prepare for this session with particular care, but I couldn't: Jack's problems had taken over my mind.

It was five p.m. when, relinquishing my study of Lewis and Clark, I rode the elevator up to my brother's twelfth-floor apartment. It had been a week since my sister and I had dropped in on him.

Two knocks. No answer. I tried again, a little harder, and pricked up my ears. Not a sound, not even the drone of the TV. I was about to use my key when the door opened partway. Jack's face was haggard, his hair disheveled.

"What do you want?" he muttered.

"Nothing," I said, edging my way into the entrance.

"I just wanted to check that everything's okay."

"Because Kid Sister sent you?"

"No. But I haven't heard from you."

That was true. For a month maybe, my brother had stopped calling to ask if I remembered the title or the words of a song, or the exact words from a book that he wanted to quote.

I took a few steps into the living room. Clothes were draped over chair-backs, books on the table, the sofa, the tops of the bookcases. The radio was on, but very low. Jack closed the door and joined me.

"What exactly do you want to know?"

"For starters, how you are."

"I'm a walking wreck but aside from that small detail, I'm fine."

His answer left me stunned. Through the French window, I contemplated the vast landscape that tenants of the Tour du Faubourg's upper floors had before their eyes. Summer was nearing its end. Far away, in the Laurentians, one could already see touches of bright red. While I was looking at the rounded mountains considered to be the oldest in the world, a flash of memory took me back to when Jack turned fifty. We hadn't fussed over that birthday; to him the start of a new decade always seemed like a death sentence.

He flopped into his chaise longue and closed his eyes. He was my brother, he looked depressed, and so I tried to find a way to draw him out. As writing was what he was happiest to talk about, I asked how his novel was coming.

"It's not the immortal masterpiece of James Fenimore Cooper," he said.

The joke wasn't new but I was reassured that he could still poke fun at himself.

"How's it coming?"

"I'm close to the end but all I can do right now is half a page before lunch. The words come *drop by drop*."

This wasn't the first time Jacques had used that expression. I was fairly sure that Hemingway had used the words to answer a journalist who was interviewing him about his private life. The famous writer had let drop that he refrained from making love whenever he had to describe intimate relations in a novel or a story. Which was tantamount to saying that the sex drive and the urge to write come from the same source.

"The words come drop by drop because I'm old," he said. "I'm fifty years old, do you realize that?"

"You are? I didn't know."

Which was a lie. To avoid hurting someone, lying is permitted. His eyes were closed. I understood that he was withdrawing into himself, so I took the risk of saying:

"Age is in people's heads."

"Are you crazy? Age is in your legs! In the morning I have trouble walking: my legs are like wood. Besides that, at mealtimes I can't eat like everybody else. When I open a TV Dinner I only eat half. I divide everything in two. I don't drink coffee or wine. My stomach can't digest anything and I spend the day making herbal teas. If you want to know, I'm ashamed of myself."

He fell silent. I wondered if the act of speaking gave him any real life or if, on the contrary, it aggravated his distress like when you scratch a wound that's itchy. Cautiously, I brought him back to the subject of writing:

"Is it something you could put in your novel?"

"Sure. But that doesn't help anything."

"What do you mean?"

"Whenever I re-read what I've written I have the impression that I've only written drivel."

"But the reviewers have nothing but praise for your books."

"That's meaningless. They say the same things about a writer I don't like."

"Are you thinking about anyone in particular?" I asked, with a hint of mischief.

"Yes."

He was thinking it over. I couldn't wait to hear what

came next. After a moment he shook his head. No luck, he'd forgotten the name of the author. He was losing his memory for names.

Abruptly, he got up.

"I think I've got his latest book."

Standing in front of the Quebec section of his library he put one knee on the ground to spare his delicate back. He ran his eyes over each shelf. At the same time, he slid his fingertips from one book to the next. And muttered. I picked up a word here and there. He was cursing authors who write a novel in two months and then visit all the radio and TV programmers. To become a media-friendly author was to him the worst sign of degradation.

"Can't find anything," he said. "My books are all mixed up, as if someone's been rooting around in my things."

He got back in his chair with a suspicious look at me. He looked despondent and I was afraid he was going to sink back into depression.

"Listen," I said. "You're doing the work you chose. You make a pretty good living. Not everybody can say that."

"You're right," he said in a phony light tone of voice. "basically I'm an old whiner. Let's just forget it. How is young Limoilou?"

"She has more self-confidence. She has a lot of character and it's a good bet that she'll soon become more independent."

"And what about the young client in a coma?"

"Last week she woke up. She looked at her boyfriend and then went back to sleep."

"While you were reading to her?"

"Yes, but…"

Jack was wide-eyed. I didn't know if it was surprise or admiration. In any case, he'd never looked at me like that before.

"You at least have a job that's good for something."

I enjoyed my work very much but I was uncertain about its effectiveness: that's what happens when you're a kid brother. I wanted to tell Jack about my concerns so he would feel less alone, but I couldn't find the right words. Meanwhile, on the radio they were playing Sylvain Lelièvre:

Can it be that as we grow old
We abandon our own hearts?

Those words touched the right chord in my brother's soul because to my dismay, all at once my brother started to cry. That hadn't happened, it seemed to me, since the day his wife had left him for a younger man.

Jack was not really crying. His shoulders were shaking and his whole body was jerking convulsively. You might have thought he was choking. He turned onto his left side in the chaise longue and pulled his knees up under his chin. I approached and after a brief hesitation I put my hand on his shoulder. He shook his head, rather brusquely so I took away my hand. I sat down at the table, on the side where you could see the mountains standing out against the grey sky.

I stayed with him until he regained his composure. Then he coughed and said rather hoarsely:

"One thing consoles me," he said.

"What's that?" I asked.

"At least I'm biodegradable."

With that strange declaration he asked me to leave and I did.

17

The Bird Woman

PARKING NEAR THE CHALET that day, I glanced towards the pond where Marine was swimming. The lovely redhead wasn't wearing a bathing suit: in her opinion the place was a corner of paradise. She did the crawl very well and she swam length after length. Now and then she would disappear beneath the surface before she reached the shore, when suddenly I would see her emerging at the other end of the pond. She avoided touching the bottom, which was muddy and silty, to keep from stirring up the water. Sitting on the dock, knees to her chin, little Limoilou was admiring the show.

I took the Lewis and Clark journal from my briefcase and rested it against the wheel of the Mini. I pretended I was re-reading it but in fact I didn't stop eying the pond below. I was waiting for the moment when Marine would emerge from the water.

Kid brothers aren't made of wood.

Since my last session of reading, Lewis and Clark had had to cope with a thousand difficulties as they advanced towards the Pacific: the backwash of the Missouri; the sandbar; the power of the current; the hordes of insects; the belligerence of some Indians. On the other hand, they had made good use of the paddlers' stamina; the experience of the French-Canadian guides and interpreters, the skill of the hunter Georges Drouillard, the good humour of the Métis Pierre Cruzatte, and the hospitality of certain tribes, such as the Mandan.

While watching Marine's prowess out of the corner of my eye, I was thinking about the warm welcome young Mandan women reserved for the members of the expedition. Each Indian woman took a visitor by the hand and led him to a teepee where she made him lie on a bison skin and lavished on him all the caresses he desired.

These images were passing through my mind when I realized, looking up, that lovely Marine had emerged from the water. Standing on the dock, her back to me, she was hopping from foot to foot, head cocked to one side: either she had water in her ears or it was to dry her long russet hair.

Limoilou wrapped her shoulders in a beach towel on which was printed a tall totem pole like those associated with some West Coast tribes. She rubbed Marine's back and kissed her cheeks. Then she gestured to let me know that she had seen me. Nearly running she went up the path that undulated between the magenta loosestrife and the orange and yellow Devil's Paintbrush. Instead of the extra large T-shirt that billowed around her, she had on pale blue jeans and a very tight white camisole she usually swam in. In the time it took me to get out of the car she was already on the steps up to the cottage and opening the screen door for me. She was barefoot.

"Hi!" she said.

"Good morning."

I pretended that I hadn't noticed her new outfit as she stepped into the solarium. Immediately, she positioned herself in front of the map that my brother had fastened to the wall: she wanted to know exactly how far the explorers had come. I showed her the site of the Mandan village on the Missouri. I though it unnecessary to talk about the favours granted by the Indian women so instead I lingered over the fact that at this campsite, Lewis and Clark had hired another French Canadian who could serve as interpreter. His name was Toussaint Charbonneau and he had several Indian wives.

"Several?" asked the astonished Limoilou.

"It was the custom," I said with a gesture of impatience. "He had at least two. The most important was Sacagawea, which means Bird-Woman."

"Right, you mentioned her."

"I'll have more to say about her but first I have to explain a couple of things."

Limoilou crossed her arms, meaning that she was listening patiently. Wasting no time I recounted the main events the members of the expedition experienced after their encounter with the Mandan.

Lewis and Clark and others had resumed their journey. Charbonneau and Sacagawea were part of it. The Indian woman was carrying a baby a few months old on her back. The explorers had at their disposal some new canoes, but navigation on the Missouri was as painful as ever. The north wind was now causing the most serious problems. One day, there was a tragedy: a squall lashed the lead craft carrying instruments, papers, medicines and articles intended for trade with the Indians. At the rudder, Charbonneau panicked and the canoe tipped on its side. The Bird Woman was flung into the cold water. Despite the powerful current, she was able to recover most of the valuable objects.

When I'd finished describing that accident, Limoilou turned towards the window. Bright-eyed, she was looking at Marine who was sunbathing on the dock with the cats. I noted with jealously that she was as interested in the Irish girl as in the exploits of the Indian woman. As usual, I pretended not to see a thing and I marked the site of the tragedy on the map. At the same time I located other stages in the explorers' journeys: the encounter with a grizzly, the great portage around the five falls of the Missouri, the Rockies, the continental divide.

"Thanks for all the details," said Limoilou as she settled onto the chaise longue. "Can I ask you something?"

"Sure."

"Will you read me what the journal says when the Bird Woman jumps into the river?"

My book was awash in bookmarks so it just took seconds to find the right place. That's how it is when you're a pro. I even had time to think about my idol, Henri Richard: three strokes of the skate and already he would be flying at top speed. He would have been proud of me. I sat in the rocking chair and read what Captain Lewis had written:

The Indian woman, in whom I recognized as much courage and resolution as would anyone at the moment of the accident, recovered most of the small articles that had been swept away by the water.

"Is that all? asked the girl.

"Yes," I said. "It's a little … stingy."

Not only that, I used the word *cheap* as if I was once again thinking that English is… Instead of belaboring that idea I tried hard to reassure Limoilou:

"You'll see, the explorers will soon change their attitude. Once they come to the foot of the Rockies, the fate of the expedition will depend on the Bird Woman."

Lewis writes:

We have come several hundred miles and now are at the heart of a mountainous region where it seems that game will soon become rare and our subsistence precarious, what with no information about the territory, not knowing how far these mountains go or where best to find a navigable branch of the Columbia.

"Can I ask you for something else?"

"Of course."

"Come closer and move your chair across from mine."

I did as she asked.

"Closer… Good, now rest your feet against mine."

She sat up in her chaise longue. That way our legs were at the same level and once my feet were resting against hers I placed my heels on the tubular edge she had just vacated. It wasn't the most comfortable position but her skin was so soft and smooth and I felt like reading for a very long time. As long as my voice didn't start quavering.

"That's perfect," she said. "Now I can't wait to hear what Bird Woman did to help the explorers. That's what you're going to tell me, right?"

"Since you're so good at guessing could you tell me what Lewis and Clark decided when they arrived at the Rockies?"

"If it was me I would decide to leave behind the canoe because in the mountains…"

She finished her remark with a funny face. Then I asked:

"But how will they transport the baggage?"

"I don't know," she said.

"I'm sorry, you can't know that. There are several things I've forgotten to tell you."

"So do it now!"

I explained briefly to Limoilou that the expedition had been prepared with the greatest care by President Thomas Jefferson. The explorers had known for a long time that to reach the Pacific they would have to pass through the Rocky Mountains. They knew as well that this climb would be possible only if they could get horses from the Shoshones.

"Did I tell you that Sacagawea was a Shoshone?"

"Yes, I think so, but I forgot."

"She'd spent her childhood around the Rockies. When still very young she had been captured by an enemy tribe and treated as a slave until Toussaint Charbonneau bought her to make her his wife."

Very discreetly I checked to see if Limoilou had reacted at all to the verb "to buy." Her eyebrows shot up but she said not a word. It was best not to mention that Charbonneau was a harsh man and that she sometimes was slapped. Instead I went on about her role in the search for the Shoshones, the horse-breeding tribe.

"They weren't there?" she asked, worried.

"No, they'd gone hunting."

"So what did she do?"

"The explorers were all upset because if they didn't get horses the expedition would be a failure. Fortunately, Bird Woman recognized places where her tribe had been going forever and everyone was reassured."

"They wrote that in their journal?"

"Of course. Wait a minute…"

I very quickly found these few lines:

On a high plain to our right the Indian woman recognized a place that in her opinion was not

107

very far from her nation's summer campground.
Her people called the hill the Beaver's Head be-
cause that was what its shape resembled.

"Then what happens?"

"They're anxious to see the Shoshone and buy horses from them, so they look for them everywhere. They also try to find a spot to cross through the mountains, I mean a path, a road, a ..."

"A notch?"

Usually Limoilou did not react so much to a reading. I must have looked astonished because she gave me a bashful smile and for my greater pleasure, she rubbed her feet against mine. To thank her I read a passage in which the Bird Woman at last found the tribe of her childhood:

They sent people to look for Sacagawea. She came,
sat, and was starting to act as interpreter when
she screamed: she had just recognized her brother
Cameahwait! She jumped up and ran to embrace
him, throwing her own blanket over him and
weeping bitter tears.

Limoilou's eyes were shining. After worrying for a moment, I realized that she was simply happy. There were streaks of light on her face. Leaving the chalet with her I was pleased with myself, my soul was light. I spotted Marine who was walking in the grass on the other side of the pond, so I waved before getting into the Mini Cooper. When she waved back the beach towel over her shoulders opened for a moment.

I remembered that image so it would keep me company on the road back to Quebec City.

18

The Famous Manuscript

WHEN MY PARENTS CHOSE my name, they had in mind a song by Félix Leclerc. The one that goes:

Francis, ton chapeau
À l'air d'une enveloppe de coco.

Whenever I wore a hat at the primary school in my village, there was always some zouave to sing that song about a hat that looks like an egg. A crowd would form around me and most of the time I had to fight. Luckily, my sister attended the same school. She would jump over the fence that separated the girls and the boys, shove the spectators out of her way, and chase away my enemy.

I was still a little boy when I heard words that I'll never forget. As usual during Christmas holidays, the house was full of company. One night when the adults were playing cards, I was sent to bed: it was much too late for children. I'm not sure of anything, maybe I was dreaming, but it seems to me that one of my uncles let it be understood that I hadn't been "wanted", that I'd arrived "by surprise." Some words stay fixed in our memories.

Long after that I talked to my sister about it. She told me that I couldn't find a better reason to carve myself a place in the sun. That was what I was trying to do. If I didn't succeed I at least discovered what I call my "life line." It runs every which way, it fluctuates between dream and reality, but it's mine. For most people reality is their prime concern. I'm not like that. I am just as happy putting my trust in someone like Monsieur Jim Harrison, when he writes: "Only our dreams give life a semblance of coherence." For some time now reality had been taking up too much space in my existence. I was helping my brother to concentrate on his story. My reading sessions had restored an appetite for life to little Limoilou. Young Alex should be leaving the hospital with a brand-new heart valve. I had been able, in appearance at least, to awaken the girl who had been in a coma after a motorcycle accident. And I'd done a good turn to a certain number of people whom I haven't yet mentioned: a young widow, a diabetic blind man, a depressed school teacher, an old man abandoned by all, some sick children, parents whose daughter had run away.

As I'd done some good work I had won the right to plunge again into the world of dream, to restore my balance. Several possibilities were available. I could repeat the hockey dream or enter those of baseball or tennis.

The baseball dream took place at Jarry Park at the time of the Expos. I came in during batting practice. Suddenly I was replacing one of the players, hitting home runs at will. The manager, Gene Mauch, appeared. When he asked me what position I played I told him I was a pitcher. He sent me to the mound and I pitched balls that did things never before seen. I struck out every batter including the very best, Rusty Staub, nicknamed le Grand Orange.

The tennis dream was set at Wimbledon. It was morning and my idol, Pete Sampras, was warming up alongside Andre Agassi. Suddenly, the ringtone of a cell phone coming from the latter's bag, could be heard. Agassi answered and from the softness of his voice you could tell that the call was from his girlfriend, Steffi Graaf, who played tennis like a dancer. It was an emergency; Agassi left for a few minutes, leaving his racquet on a chair. Then I stepped onto the court. I picked up the racquet, I played against Sampras, and I beat him six-love.

My three dreams—hockey, baseball, tennis—were like old companions, and I liked them because I could always change the duration, replace one person with another, make any change I wanted. This time though I wanted to invent a new space for dreaming. I lay on my bed in the fetal position and I closed my eyes. Little by little I made up the following story.

I was with my sister. We were at the old Musée de l'Amérique française, at the entrance to the Petit Séminaire in Vieux-Québec. By my watch it was 4:55 p.m. We would be pushing the door open five minutes before closing; everything was going as anticipated. My sister went in first and I was hard on her heels. The guards had left the museum, the only person left was the attendant at the reception desk. A timid-looking young man. The keys were on the counter in front of him.

My sister stepped up and, leaning over the counter, positioned herself right across from him. She had unbuttoned her shirt, her generous curves were overflowing a little, that was our plan. The young man made an effort to look her in the eyes, but he couldn't stop himself from blinking. All was well. My sister said she just wanted to take a quick look in the first gallery. He peered at the clock but she held him by the hand and led him off, murmuring very sweet words to him. Meanwhile, I was using the keys to open the sliding door of a display cabinet that contained a metal box. It was the object we had set our hearts on. I grabbed it, then put the keys back on the counter and hurried out of the museum.

It was agreed that my sister would figure out on her own how to make the attendant unaware the box had disappeared. We would take it back first thing the next day after we'd photographed the precious documents inside for old Jack. We wanted to help my brother finish his novel about French America.

In my dream, the box held a treasure: Louis Jolliet's famous manuscript. The journal he had written after his return from the great journey on the Mississippi with Father Marquette, that he had lost forever in a shipwreck on the rapids at Lachine.

19

Fall Colours

ON MY WAY to the cottage that day I didn't know what to expect. It was Marine who had invited me. It couldn't be about reading to Limoilou: it was midweek. I was intrigued, but also very happy at the prospect of seeing the lovely redhead whose image had obsessed me since my last visit.

The two girls were waiting for me on the front steps. Each had a cat on her knees. Limoilou was in jeans and a hoodie, and Marine had on a skirt and a turtleneck in fall colours. Now, in late morning, the air was still cool. A bit of grey smoke was coming from the chimney.

The cats ran away at the sight of the Mini Cooper. When the girls got up to welcome me I sensed that something unusual was brewing. It was the first time I'd seen Marine in a skirt. I didn't feel very comfortable. In the Canadiens' locker room, Henri Richard was keeping his eyes on the ground.

"Don't worry," said Marine.

I was about to reply that I was not at all worried, but Limoilou smiled at me with such candor that I stopped myself just in time. The girls took turns greeting me with a kiss, then they invited me in. The table was covered with a blue-and-white checkered tablecloth spread with all sorts of hors d'oeuvre, sandwiches cut into triangles and a big bowl of salad with ham and fruit. To avoid doing things like everyone else, I refrained from the usual question: "To what do I owe the honour?" While we were eating I was the object of a great deal of attention and I realized they wanted to thank me for my reading sessions. The girls' kindness warmed my heart, especially as they didn't stop filling my glass of rosé wine.

My thoughts were all muddled. They were gently making fun of me when I muttered that I really was keen to do the dishes. Marine's green eyes never left mine and wrapped me in their warmth. I was fascinated but I couldn't say precisely what she had in mind.

All of a sudden Limoilou got up and said she was going for a walk. She wanted to go down the winding path to the riverbank and spend a little time with the retired race horses. As she had tons of things to tell them, she was liable to be gone until late afternoon.

Marine suggested coffee. My head was spinning and I accepted gratefully. I followed her unsteadily into the kitchen. The coffee was strong. I had two cups but it wasn't enough to bring me back down to earth. Then she took me by the hand and led me into her bedroom, made me lie down on her bed. I was somewhat surprised. It was hard not to think about the invitations from the Indian women of the Mandan tribe. When she bent over me to take off my shoes her long hair tumbled onto my legs. Through the fog in my brain I realized that this girl who was my age had always attracted me. I hadn't dared to admit it; first of all, she was my brother's friend, and then she had a hot-tempered personality that scared me.

When she reached out to straighten the pillow, I took her hand. I brushed it with my lips as they did in olden times. It seemed to me that her eyes were telling me tender words. I pulled slightly on her arm and at the same time I moved aside to clear some space for her in the bed. She lay down beside me.

"Bonjour, little brother!" she said cheerfully.

"Bonjour!"

She turned onto her side, legs flexed. Pushed her hair aside so it fell onto her back. Then she placed one hand between her knees, hitching up her skirt, and slipped the other one under the pillow.

"Who are you?" she asked, still in the same tone of voice.

"I don't know exactly."

"Because of the rosé?"

"Yes, but not just that."

There was infinite patience in her eyes, while I tried for several minutes to clarify my thoughts. My efforts came to naught. Finally she suggested:

"Do you feel like telling me what you're thinking?"

"I can try," I said.

She half-closed her eyes and then, taking her hand out from under the pillow, she placed it with the one that was between her knees. That movement pulled her skirt a little higher but I acted as if I'd seen nothing.

"Was the invitation because of my reading?"

"Of course."

"That's very nice. But you know, something unexpected has happened."

"Oh yes?"

"You told me that reading was a kind of therapy. Do you remember? It was at the beginning of summer."

"I remember. And?"

"Well, it seems that the therapy worked in both directions. Limoilou has changed, but she's not the only one: I've changed too."

Marine freed her right hand to stroke my cheek and under my chin, then put it back between her knees.

"How have you changed?"

"It's hard to say. And I have no idea where to start."

"Say the first thing that comes into your mind."

"Okay… like there were several persons in me."

"Several?"

In my head the fog was dissipating. I made an effort to reflect.

"No, I didn't express myself properly. I meant: everyone I've talked about in my reading is part of me now. Do you understand?"

"I think so."

I in turn stroked her cheek as delicately as possible. She closed her eyes. I tried to go on with the explanation but my heart was beating too fast and the words came out all tangled. Yet what I was thinking about wasn't so complicated. I was thinking about Charbonneau, Drouillard, Cruzatte, and all the others, the obscure and the nonentities; about the great explorers, Jolliet, La Salle, and La Vérendrye; and even about my father, who was capable of building a house. About all those people, what I meant was that a little of their blood, mixed with some Indian blood, flowed in my veins. I had put off realizing it. It was the reading sessions that had enhanced my awareness and made me think.

Marine was now watching me closely and I could

see that she was trying to read my thoughts. I waited for her to say something but instead she slipped one hand inside my sweater. Maybe she was trying to tell me that it was better to use gestures rather than words to resolve certain problems. I shared her opinion, especially because her hand was nice and warm, but I had to talk a little about Jack because I had the feeling I was taking his place.

"Don't rack your brains," she said. "I have an understanding with him."

"Thank you, thanks very much," I said simply.

"That's all right."

"May I say another couple of things?"

"Of course."

"Jack has nearly finished his book. He's found a title: *l'Anglais n'est pas une langue magique.* It's something he heard me say.'"

"Weird title for a novel…"

"That's what I told him. He replied that French was the magic language, that he showed that in his book, and that I had proven it myself with my reading sessions."

Marine made no reply. Her hand moved down towards my belly, with little detours. I said again:

"As long as he hasn't finished his book, my sister and I will look after him. And that's it. No, one more thing:… Jack isn't very happy with his novel. He blames himself for using a book written in English, the journal of Lewis and Clark, to show the position occupied in America by the French… Okay, that's all I have to say."

She gave me a very sweet smile, looking calmly at me as if we had the whole day ahead of us. After a long moment she brought her face close to mine and kissed me on the mouth. I slipped my hands under her sweater. Her breasts were bare, warm, and firm. She purred like a cat. Then she pulled my sweater over my head. I took hers off too, carefully because of the turtleneck, and touched with my lips on all the spaces I had yet to discover.

There was nothing aggressive in what we were doing, only caresses and laughter. Marine was softer than I'd expected. She took off all my clothes and I removed hers. And the rest happened by itself, or almost, as if I were being pushed by the people who had come before me, my father and all the others. I even took the initiative and slowed my movements because I wanted the pleasure to never end.

Finally, I wasn't sure that I was still a kid brother.

20

The Little Reader

LIMOILOU WAS WITH me in the Mini Cooper.

We were transporting some of her baggage and a plastic bag of books. She had turned back towards the chalet several times as the car was climbing the dirt road that led to the main one. I was thinking about the Léo Ferré song, *Si tu t'en vas.*

We were driving along the Chemin Royal towards Quebec City. It was Indian Summer. I was driving slowly to give Limoilou time to see my favourite places. The peaceful cemetery where people left their shoes on the grave of Félix Leclerc. An ancestral house with a shingle roof and blue windows, *L'isle de Bacchus* that was hidden in the trees as if by humility. The bridge to the island that opened like a stage curtain before the great Montmorency Falls.

On the Dufferin autoroute, I took the slowest lane.

The sand bars were covered with wild geese. With her legs folded under her, Limoilou was swaying back and forth. Her eyes sparkled and her head was turned to the left to admire the river, then to the right to watch the people pedaling along the bicycle path. In the distance stood the imposing silhouette of the Château Frontenac, the tower of the Parliament, and the downtown luxury hotels.

I was careful not to brush against her knee when I was handling the gear shift to turn right on d'Aiguillon. Two intersections further we were at the garage of the Tour du Faubourg. Just as I was unlocking the door I turned around to see if Bogie's Shadow was nearby. It wasn't there. Ever since my sister's intervention, the Mounties had left me alone. Maybe they had given up the investigation because the mysterious woman, as in my sleeping dream, had gone back to the Old Continent.

After parking the Mini in my reserved space, I took Limoilou's baggage and her bag of books out of the trunk. We went up to the second floor. Her small apartment appealed to him right away and one part of my fears vanished. Instead of unpacking she announced that first, she wanted to deal with her books. I took the books, picked up the plastic bag with the Vaugeois Bookstore, logo and we left. On the main floor I checked discreetly to be sure the building key was in my pocket. We exited through the door that opened onto rue Saint-Jean.

Limoilou was hesitating over which way to go. To give her time to think, I looked at the books. There were four. A moment later she pulled me towards the left. Across from the pharmacy she crossed the street, and I followed her into the cemetery of the old St. Matthew's Church. I sat on a bench, the books beside me, while she wandered among the graves.

It was an ambiguous place. The cemetery had been converted into a public garden where people came for a rest or even for a bite to eat at noon, but everywhere there were gravestones, standing or lying, upon which names and dates could be read. And how could I forget that Marine's Irish mother and grandmother had been buried behind the church, in the most secluded corner?

It was only 10 a.m., it was hard for the sun to break through the rusty foliage. We weren't alone in the cemetery: a group of punks, two guys and a girl, were playing with a pit bull. They were dressed in black with metal ornaments and I was afraid the presence of these young people might remind Limoilou of painful episodes in her past, but my fears were unfounded. She came and joined me without even looking at them. Maybe I was something of a mother hen.

After spreading out the books on my bench she chose *The Call of the Wild*, by Monsieur Jack London.

I saw her walk straight to a bronze statue in a corner of the church. It was a sculpture by Lewis Pagé of a young girl sitting bent forward with her legs crossed and all her attention focussed on a book she was holding in both hands. Incongruously, the book's shape was barely roughed out. You might have thought it was a box. Limoilou placed London's novel in the trash can.

"That might warm someone's heart," she said, rejoining me.

I thought she was going to say why she had chosen this book but she made her way in silence to the stairs that looked down on rue Saint-Joachim. In my memory, Jack London told the story of a dog that had been abused by some men seeking gold in the Yukon, that eventually regained its freedom: that's all I remember.

Limoilou turned left onto the ruelle des Augustines, then right on Saint-Patrick. Her little smile told me her route was not accidental.

She stopped in front of a playground for young children at the corner of rue Scott. There were games in every colour of plastic: slides, ladders, swings.

She sat on the edge of the sidewalk. I joined her and, taking out the books, I arranged them between us. Without hesitating she chose *The Road to Altamont,* a collection of short stories by Madame Gabrielle Roy.

This time, I asked:

"Is it because of the little girl in that story 'The Old Man and the Child'? The one who wants to see Lake Winnipeg?"

"That's right."

She got up, pushed open a black metal gate and entered the playground. I had read and re-read the story. The heroine was eight or ten years old. She was looking for a sign of an old man who often sat under a tree because of the heat. When he mentioned Lake Winnipeg to the little girl, the old man said: "You can't see from one shore to the other." One day the two of them took the train to see that vast expanse of water and the journey was so well described that at the end, the lake became the very symbol of happiness.

Limoilou set the book at the top of the highest slide. Then we went down rue Scott, which was very steep. Just as we were turning right on Saint-Jean, bus number 7 revved its engine and stopped farther away, brakes squealing. Instinctively, Limoilou pressed herself against me, her head sunk deep into her shoulders.

I'll have to get used to noise again," she said.

"You'll get there, "I said. "It won't take long."

"Thanks. You're a sweetheart."

She began to smile. Her confidence was coming back.

"I'm glad to be in the city."

The apartment Marine and I had found for her, on the first floor of the Tower, had just one room and a half. Later we would go with her to look for a more comfortable quarters in the neighbourhood, and probably a part-time job.

"For sure I'm going to miss Marine," she said.

"Me too," I murmured.

"And I'm going to miss my cat."

"We'll go to see them whenever you want."

There was a glimmer in her eyes, all was well. The sky was dark blue, and it was getting warmer so she pulled off her sweater and tied it around her waist. The scars on her wrists were less visible now. She started walking again and stopped almost at once.

We were in front of the store *Le copiste du faubourg*. It was the stationery store where old Jack bought everything he needed for writing. The house had a pretty roof with pale blue dormer windows that extended to the frames of the display windows. They held ballpoints, pens, staplers, as well as all kinds of notebooks, scribblers, scratchpads. From them emanated a sense of privacy, almost of solitude. You thought of someone writing in a corner of his bedroom.

There were now only two books in my bag. Limoilou

opted for *Salut Galarneau*, by Monsieur Jacques God-bout. I quite liked that novel because it had a style. More-over, it seemed to have been written especially for me: the narrator was named François, and his brother Jacques, a writer, lived at the top of a tower.

Limoilou set down the book on the last of the four steps at the entrance, resting it against the display win-dow on the right. She didn't want customers to trip on their way out of the shop. Looking satisfied she took my arm to cross rue Saint-Jean again, in the middle of the traffic. Then she turned left on rue Sainte-Marie, which led to the lower town below. A few moments later her hand felt heavier, her face clouded over. You didn't have to be a great psychologist to understand what was going on: we were entering the part of town where she had lived her most painful experiences.

"Are you all right?" I asked.

"Yes," she said. "Don't worry."

Now she was the one reassuring me. I was slightly ashamed but I remembered all too well what Marine and Jack had told me: the suicide attempt, the ambu-lance siren, the visits to Hôtel-Dieu hospital, the con-valescence.

I struggled to drive away the old images.

We were at the corner of Richelieu.

"Nearly there!" she said to encourage me. She was heading for a small park adjacent to the Blanchet shoe store parking lot. It consisted of nothing but a few benches arranged around a group of birches. As far as she knew, it was one of the rare places in the neighbourhood where one could find trees. I handed her the last book: *Lumière des oiseaux*, by Monsieur Pierre Morency. The cover showed a great blue heron with its long yellow bill, its intent gaze, and the black feather that floated behind its tucked-in neck.

Limoilou set the book on a bench, then turned towards me.

"There, that's it," she said. "I've done what I wanted to do. Thank you for coming with me."

Standing on tiptoe, she kissed me on the cheek. Then took my arm again and declared that she couldn't wait to settle into her apartment. We got back to the Tour du Faubourg. I was both happy to see that everything was going well and worried because I wondered if I would have the patience to look after her. Counting on Jack was not really possible: dissatisfied with the novel he'd just finished he had started another that he didn't want to talk about for the moment.

One thing reassured me though. Marine, who was very attached to Limoilou, was going to come to Quebec

City more often. I knew a little brother who couldn't wait to hold her in his arms. He dreamed of it day and night.

When I got home after helping Limoilou settle in, I saw that there was a message on my voice mail. My day had been rich in emotions so I first went to the kitchen. While I was making coffee my imagination wandered off. Was it my brother already questioning himself about his new novel? The lovely Irish girl asking for news? Another mysterious woman suggesting a meeting?

Sources

37: Map, City of Paris, *Petit Larousse*, 1997; 44 Map, Donald Jackson, *Thomas Jefferson and the Stony Mountains: Exploring the West from Monticello*, University of Oklahoma Press, 1993; 69: Book cover, *Far West: Journal de la première traversée du continent nord-américain, 1804-1806*, Phébus Libretto, 1993; 64 Alain Grandbois, *Les îles de la nuit*, Éditions Typo, 1994, S. Fischman, trans.; 81-83: Réjean Ducharme, *L'Avalée des avalé*, Éditions Gallimard, S. Fischman, trans.; 87: lyrics of *Fais comme si,* by Michel Rivegauche sung by Édith Piaf in the film *Les amants de demain* (1959) directed by Marcel Blistène; 98: From the song "Qu'est-ce qu'on a fait de nos rêves?" by Sylvain Lelièvre; 110: From the song *Francis* written and sung by Félix Leclerc; 121: Jim Harrison, *The Road Home* (1998), Atlantic Monthly Press; 126: From Gabrielle Roy, *La route d'Altamont* (1966), HMH.

43-44, 67-68, 70-73, 104-105, 108: *Journals of the Lewis and Clark Expedition.*

ESPLANADE
Books

THE FICTION SERIES AT VÉHICULE PRESS

A House by the Sea : A novel by Sikeena Karmali

A Short Journey by Car : Stories by Liam Durcan

Seventeen Tomatoes : Tales from Kashmir : Stories by Jaspreet Singh

Garbage Head : A novel by Christopher Willard

The Rent Collector : A novel by B. Glen Rotchin

Dead Man's Float : A novel by Nicholas Maes

Optique : Stories by Clayton Bailey

Out of Cleveland : Stories by Lolette Kuby

Pardon Our Monsters : Stories by Andrew Hood

Chef : A novel by Jaspreet Singh

Orfeo : A novel by Hans-Jürgen Greif
[Translated by Fred A. Reed]

Anna's Shadow : A novel by David Manicom

Sundre : A novel by Christopher Willard

Animals : A novel by Don LePan

Writing Personals : A novel by Lolette Kuby

Niko : A novel by Dimitri Nasrallah

Stopping for Strangers : Stories by Daniel Griffin

The Love Monster: A novel by Missy Marston

A Message for the Emperor : A novel by Mark Frutkin

New Tab : A novel by Guillaume Morissette

Swing in the House : Stories by Anita Anand

Breathing Lessons : A novel by Andy Sinclair

Ex-Yu : Stories by Josip Novakovich

The Goddess of Fireflies : A novel by Geneviève Pettersen
[Translated by Neil Smith]

All That Sang : A novella by Lydia Perović

English is Not a Magic Language : A novel by Jacques Poulin
[Translated by Sheila Fischman]

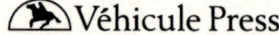 Véhicule Press